A CROSS TO BEAR BOOK 6

KATHI S. BARTON

This is a work of fiction. Names, characters, places, and incidents are products of the author's imagination or are used fictitiously and are not to be construed as real. Any resemblance to actual events, locations, organizations, or persons, living or dead, is entirely coincidental.

World Castle Publishing, LLC
Pensacola, Florida
Copyright © 2024 Kathi S. Barton
Hardback ISBN: 9798300078744
Paperback ISBN: 9798891263130
eBook ISBN: 9798891263147
First Edition World Castle Publishing, LLC, November 18, 2024
http://www.worldcastlepublishing.com
Licensing Notes
Cover: Karen Fuller
Editor: Karen Fuller

Chapter 1

Ewing was keeping an eye on the kids while he changed Billy's diaper. He'd been getting really good at changing the boy's diaper since he and the other children came to him. But with six kids, he knew that something could change in a heartbeat, and he'd be right back to square one in learning an entirely new set of rules and standards for them all. He thought that this was the hardest job he'd ever held. And the one with the most benefits.

Two weeks ago—he couldn't believe that it had only been a couple of weeks now. He'd been out taking a walk on his property checking on things and came upon a man stealing his grape starters for the new wine he was planning. At first his plan had been to scare him off, call the police perhaps. But in the end, he'd done so much more than that.

The man, Ben Kinsley, a bastard of a man had two little girls with him that looked like not only could they use a good bath but a good meal too. As soon as he'd spoken to the man, one of the children, Beth, came running to him and hid behind his legs. He and his bear both could feel her terror. It was all he could do not to kill the man where he stood when the other child, another six-year-old, Rachel, came toward him only to be knocked down and stomped on by the bastard. By the time his brothers showed up, he had them both with him and was ready to become their knight in shining armor for anything that they needed.

"What do you 'pose they're going to do with us today?" He asked Lily, the most worldly seven-year-old he knew what she meant and what reason. "You said this man is going to decide if we can live with you and your family or not until they find the other kids' parents. What happens if they don't?"

"You'll stay with me, I hope." She asked him if he was nuts. "Sometimes I think that I am, but we're doing all right, aren't we? I mean, nothing bad has happened, and so far, I've been able to keep you all alive and fed."

"Yeah, you're doing good about that, but I heard that lady in the bathroom telling her friend that you needed a wife and shouldn't be taking little girls to the bathroom. I don't know how she expects us to get all our bits and pieces covered up without you there. All she did was lift her nose at us." He didn't comment even though he'd heard the woman talking, too. "You think that you'll get you a wife, and she'll be all right with all of us?"

"She will." She eyed him like he was a spot on her new dress. "She will. I know it. And if I do have a mate out there, I'm not going to drop you like a hot potato because some woman has a burr up her bottom about me having six kids."

"Uncle Mark said that you were a good man. I didn't want to believe him, but I think you're the best." He kissed her on the cheek and told he that he loved her as well. "Don't get all sappy on me. You know how I hate that crap."

It was their turn to go in and see the judge. All five of the little girls, each one of them a stair step down from the first child, Patty, who was also the oldest. At eight, she'd been hurt more than most people had their entire lives. Both mentally and physically. Once they were seated, the new rule he'd given them, they sat on their hands and didn't touch each other. They meant no harm when doing that, not that they were teasing one another either, but some of the children were still healing, and touching one of the many wounds would cause a meltdown. He sat little Billy in his car seat on the seat next to him while he slept through his first nap of the day.

After making sure that the first two children he'd gotten that night were taken care of then little Billy came to him. The infant, only a couple of weeks old then, wouldn't have made it had it not been for the magic of the women that were in the family nor the bits of blood that he gave the baby too. Billy had been too long without anyone ever caring for him. At four weeks old, he weighed less than the normal nine to nine and a half pounds a one-month-old should weigh. However, he was getting bigger daily.

The next three children, little girls, all of them with blond curly hair and varying shades of blue eyes, were brought to the hospital after finding them in an abandoned home with nothing for them to eat, much less drink, when they too were brought to him. They'd been together since, and he wondered daily what he was going to do without them if the judge told him he wasn't fit to be a father — a single father to them any longer. The door behind him opened, and he saw his family coming in. He asked Mark, his older brother, what he was doing here.

"You didn't think we'd let you have all the fun, did you? He hugged them all and was happy when his five sisters-in-law hugged him as well. Ewing was much too busy keeping the kids quiet when the door behind them opened once again, and a group of others came into the room. He told Mark how worried he was. "You've got this little brother. Don't worry. I promise you, you've got this."

Ewing certainly hoped so. There were days that he wasn't sure he was doing the right thing with these kids. Then one of them would come up to him and hug him, and he'd be all right until the next near catastrophe came along to have him worrying once again.

There really had been some near misses, too. Once, when he'd decided that he needed to just pop into the shower and get ready for the day, one of the kids decided that they'd simply make breakfast for the rest of the kids that were up. It was a mess, and he was still finding batter on walls when she'd burnt her little finger on the stove. No one had ended up in the hospital, nor had anyone had him arrested so he wasn't sure what kind of disaster he was waiting on to befall them all.

After standing up and then having a seat when the judge entered, he realized that they weren't the only ones in the courthouse today to get things cleared away. Making sure that the girls were all right, he thought about the work that was getting more behind every day at home. Ewing wondered if he'd been smart or not in asking the faeries to help him with his grapes. These were the faeries that his family took care of and they would be able to get all the grapes tied up to the wires that held the vines up. He usually did all the work himself in a day or two, but there just hadn't been any time for much more than the kids in a while. When one of the kids poked him, he turned to look where she pointed.

"Do you know that man?" He grinned and told Harper that he was the president. "Of what? He sure does dress fancy."

"The United States, honey. Pay attention.

This might be good for whoever he's here for."
She rolled her eyes at him, something that he was
getting fairly familiar with, having little girls in
his home. It could mean one of several things,
but he thought that the one being used right now
as that he was in over his head. Again. He didn't
particularly care for that look but since he felt like
that most of the time, he didn't disagree with her.
Ewing was asked to stand, and he was barely able
to get up before his beautiful little girls stood up as
well in their seats.

"You're not gonna hurt him." He told Beth
that he had this. "I don't care who he is. He's not
gonna hurt you. You're all I gots."

"You have all those children surrounding
you as well as the family here behind you, isn't
that right?" The Judge, Fred Hartman, asked Beth
to sit down, but she was on a roll. "What's your
name, little girl? I should have it here, but I don't...
can you please tell me your name, honey?"

"Beth Carter Cross, but I don't like the Carter
part." The judge told her that he could understand
that. "No, you can't. No body that wasn't with
us can understand the stuff that we've had to do
because our parents weren't fit to have a puppy."

Then Patty started talking.

"I was going to do this my own way after we voted on it last night—" Patty glared at Beth. "Anyway, we voted and we don't want to ever leave here without Mr. Ewing. He's been so good to us that I'm about to pop a button or two. And you know what? I have buttons to pop. We didn't have not a single sock when we were trapped up inside that nasty house. None of us even had an idea that we'd be around the next day the way those people kept bringing us in and out cages." She leaned down when Lily spoke to her then Patty looked at the judge. "I'm supposed to tell you that we want to adopt Mr. Ewing as our daddy. I know he's not but he sure did take us into his house that day. He even says that he loves us. Nobody ever said that to us before him. We get to have baths and food and he even took us all out to a restaurant. I don't know that he's going to do that again, but up until that lady yelled at us for hogging up the bathroom, it was going right well."

Ewing laughed, and so did the judge and the president. But it was Shippley, Mr. President, that started speaking.

"I don't know that I could have said it better

myself, young lady. And I heard about the woman yelling at the lot of you. I think I might have been more upset with her than Ewing was." Patty asked if they could stay. "That's not up to me, but this judge right here. And if it matters at all, I couldn't recommend anyone better for the job than Ewing here. He not only has the patience of a saint with them but also the backing of his family to do right by these children. If my opinion matters, that is."

He didn't know who was more impressed with the vote of confidence, the judge or himself. But Patty apparently wasn't satisfied with that answer and told him to tell her what she had to do to get to stay with him. The judge cleared his throat, amused that things were going in this direction, Ewing thought.

"We've had very little luck in finding your parents, Miss Patty. I also have it here that Miss Beth and Miss Rachel's parents are all no longer with us. Young Billy…well, it looks like his parents have no desire to raise him either. The only ones that I do have a bead on are Miss Harper and Miss Lily." He looked at Patty before going on. "I'm going to talk to you as you've been talking with me, young lady, and tell you that all you children will continue to live with the Cross family, Ewing as the main person that will answer for you until such time as we can get to the bottom of the mess that is the families in this thing. Does that mean that he can adopt you today? No, I'm sorry, it does not. But I do know that as soon as I know something, you will as well."

"Can we call him daddy?" The judge looked at him just as he was wiping the tears off his cheeks. He told her that would be up to Ewing but he'd bet he'd not mind. "He's the best, Mr. Judge. The other night…well, I had me an accident. I was having a bad dream, and he was right there for me. Didn't cuff me upside the head like my parents would have, and didn't take away none of my food. He just helped me to clean up and while I was taking a shower, he made sure my bed was clean and dried off so I could go back to sleep. He never one time said anything to anyone. I won't go back to that other kind of house, Mr. Judge. I've…we all love him so much and want to stay with him forever."

He held Patty while she sobbed to him about how it wasn't fair. That people shouldn't have children if they were going to be mean to them. For five minutes, there wasn't a dry eye in the room. He himself was hurting so badly for the children that were in his care that he might well have run off with them if anyone was coming for them.

By the time the adoption paperwork for the other four children was completed, they were all exhausted. Billy was doing the best, he supposed, since he seemed to be able to sleep through just about anything but the girls. His girls were so tired even the prospect of having lunch with their favorite uncles and aunts wasn't enough to pull them out of their funk.

He hoped that tomorrow would be better. However if anyone asked, he wasn't counting on it. Ewing had to leave the kids with a sitter for a few hours later this evening to go to the vineyard and check on things. It was a test of sorts to see how much work he could get done without them there to distract him.

He was so happy that he'd found a friend in the Applegate family through their daughter Pauline Dixon, whom he'd met at the hospital. The family provided him with endless hand-me-downs as well as advice that he couldn't get from his family as he was the only one that had all girls but for Billy and the only one with an infant. Just then, he decided that he needed a good long nap.

~*~

Liza asked again why it was her that had to go to the Cross house to babysit. She still didn't have an answer, but she was willing to bet that no one wanted to do it because the kids were brats. She said as much to her older sister, Pauline.

"I've told you this several times, Liza. They're wonderful children, and they have a good father in Ewing." She told her that they probably had all the gizmos in the world. "Doubtful any of them have much more than the clothing on their backs. Why are you being such a bitch about this? Christ, I would have loved to have been able to babysit a rich man's kids for a couple of hours and make the kind of bucks he's talking about."

"He'll more than likely sue me or something if one of them gets a simple splinter." Liza knew she was being a bitch, but she had wanted to go to the mall with her friends, not babysit. Besides, there was a cute guy at the movie theater that she wanted to get to know, too. She looked up when Shelby, the second older sister, came into the room. "I have to sit for the Cross kids."

"Good for you. I hear that poor Mr. Cross hasn't been out doing anything since he got them. They're supposed to be these really nice kids, too." She said that it was also more than likely a lie concocted because they had money. "Oh, grow up. You're sixteen. Get your head out of your ass and go sit the kids. You might enjoy it."

"Doubtful that anyone would enjoy watching six kids with money." Shelby asked her if she was pissed off because they had money. "Yes. I'm betting that he only pays about ten bucks an hour for me to go there. I will miss out on fun at the mall and be made fun of because I'm stuck there. I need to get away from this family. Why would anyone think that it's all right to volunteer anyone for a sitting job when they know that I have a life."

"You're sixteen, as I said. You're not entitled to a life just yet. Mom volunteered you because you said that you wanted money this summer. Well, you'll get it this way." She stomped her foot while leaving the kitchen, where her sister was laughing at her. "What are you going to do when he gives you fifty bucks? Complain about that, too?"

"I'll go." She looked at her sister Megan when she came into the kitchen. "Mom said that you were being a brat and that since you think you're too good to go babysit for the nicest family around, I'll do it."

"Really?" She nodded, pulling off her sweatshirt in favor of the warmer weather. "Really, and for truly, you'll do this?"

"I said that I would, didn't I? Besides, it will be the perfect way for me to get out of the house and make a few bucks for my next quarter in college. I'm sure that you would be mean to the kids simply because you don't want to be there." She told her sister that she would not. "Sure you won't. Like you weren't mean to Clay when you watched him for only fifteen minutes. However, if I make some really good bucks off of this, I'm going to rub it in your face for all eternity."

"Good. I'm so glad that you'll do this for me." Liza was making plans even before she pulled out her cell phone to call her friends. One of the girls had an older brother, Devlin, who was going to be dropping them off at the mall, and she couldn't have been more happy. She didn't even feel guilty for her sister taking over the dreaded job because she was going to have herself some fun. "Can I borrow ten bucks in case we can go to the movies?"

No one in the house would lend her even enough money to get her a cola while the others had pizza at the mall. Family sucked, and she would be so thrilled when she was old enough to leave home.

Liza only had a couple more years, and she'd be free. Once she was, she wasn't ever coming back to this stupid town, even for funerals. Well, maybe for a funeral, but nothing else. They all sucked as far as she was concerned.

By the time she was picked up, she'd made enough phone calls to let everyone know that she'd been set free. Posting selfies of herself on the web had her doing kissy faces to her followers. Getting into the car, something else that she was going to own soon, they were all headed to the one place where she could be free and herself.

The mall around here wasn't the one that the tourists liked to visit. It was a little more run-down than the one just outside of town, but it was a place that didn't cater to the stupid and boring people who came to the park a million times a year. She was excited too that the movie theater guy was sitting in one of the big seats outside the movie place and was smoking a cigarette.

"Here, have a hit." It wasn't a cigarette at all but some pot. Telling the guy—he was even more handsome this close that she didn't want any had her friends and Vance, the guy, making fun of her. She didn't want anything to do with drugs. Her family would kill her if they found out, and she knew that they would, and she'd never be able to go out again.

"Come on, Liza. Just take a little. It'll get you all relaxed." Liza was good at ignoring peer pressure. Simply telling them no had worked before, but this time, it was in front of Vance. Shaking her head she could feel her resolve waning and wondered if she was going to be able to say no all night. "You're a big baby. What are they going to do, smell it on you? By the time we're headed home, you'll be all right, and we'll have had a good time."

"No." She finally walked away, her heart pounding in her chest enough to make her feel like she was in trouble. Vance came to sit next to her, and he told her it was all right. "I just don't want to get into trouble. You have no idea how hard it is to have so many sisters and brothers, and they know your every move. Just stop it. All right?"

When she looked at him, he blew smoke in her face. For a few seconds, no more, she felt good, but that soon wore off, and she felt a pinch to her arm. Turning to yell at the person who had hurt her, she was falling off the chair and onto the mall's dirty floor. The syringe in his hands made her so terrified that she didn't know what to do now.

"You just had to keep saying no, didn't you? Stupid bitch. You're not going to fuck up my ability to make a little more cash." She could hear voices; however, she wasn't able to respond to them. Her mouth felt nasty, and her entire body felt like it didn't belong to her. "We'll have to carry her. She's too fucking stupid to just do what others told her. Put them in the trunk with that kid Devlin. Moron. Thought he could take me on when we knew what we were doing. As for this bitch," The kick to her ribs had her crying out. "Put her in the trunk, too. It's all she deserves for making me have to drug her up."

She was helped to the car by being dragged. Liza could see the other girls that she hung out with. Each of them, too, was being dragged out of the mall. Terror like she'd never felt before made her sick to her stomach, and just as she was getting her feet under her, she felt another pinch to her arm, and she was out.

The next time that she woke up she was in complete darkness. Knowing on some level that she was in the trunk of a car didn't make her feel all that much better about her situation. Being where she thought she was made her ill again. The smell of someone who had puked was close to her, and she couldn't move with the weight of something or someone atop her. Trying to get to her cell phone, she nearly sobbed when she found it in her pocket. She couldn't get it to her mouth, now with all the weight on her, so she dialed what she hoped was 911 so she could get out of there.

"Ewing Cross." She started to hang up but didn't know if she'd get to call anyone else. Pulling the phone as close to her as she could get it, she could see that she had about eleven percent battery left. "Hello? Is anyone—"

"I'm about out of battery. I've been kidnapped from the mall. I think that there are…I don't know. Three people with me. Can you call my mommy for me?" Feeling stupid because she'd called her mom mommy, she tried her best to concentrate on what he was saying to her. "I'll babysit for you forever if you get me. Please, Mr. Cross. Can you find me?"

"You said you were at the mall. Which one?" She told him. "How did you get there, and do you know if the car you're in is the one you arrived in."

"One of the girls with me, she's been puking so that's all I know about the car." She looked around the best she could. "One of the tail lights is just a hole in the car. I don't know what that means, but if that helps."

"Can you hear anything? Is it a rough motor? Can you hear other cars? Does it feel like you're going really fast?" She didn't know and started crying. "Pay attention to me." His voice was hard like she'd pissed him off, and so did what he said. "Listen. What do you hear?"

She was smashed up against one of the girls she had been with, and it felt like she wasn't breathing. Of course, she couldn't tell, not where she was, but she hoped they were all right. Listening to pay attention to her surroundings, she could hear car horns as well as the swishing of something going by her super-slow. She told the man that.

"Good. You're on a back road and not the highway. Where were you in the mall? How did they get you out of there without you fighting them?" She told him that they'd been at the movie end of the mall and that a man by the name of Vance was the one who had given her something. "All right, that helps. I'm almost there now. Just keep calm. I know that you're a shifter, but I don't know that I've ever known what."

"Cougars. My mom isn't, but my dad and most of my brothers and sisters are. I'm going to die, aren't I, Mr. Cross? I was so stupid that I just wanted to leave my family, and now I might not see them again." He told her to behave and that he was pulling into the mall parking lot now. "I'm not there. I tried to tell you that. They took me out—"

"I'm trying to get your scent." She felt stupid as soon as he told her what was going on. "My sister has some dogs that will be able to find you faster, so I'm calling her now. Don't hang up. I'm also going to call your family." She nodded, then remembered that he couldn't see her. "Hang on. And no more thoughts of dying. I'm working on it. Just…don't hang up. If I don't hear from you or we get lost, I'm going to find you."

She didn't ask him if he was going to find her alive or not but did worry about that. She also told herself that she wasn't going to go to the mall without her family ever again. If she ever got to go to the mall, that was. She was being whiney and hated herself for that.

It seemed like forever before she heard from Ewing. But before she could ask him how the search was going, the trunk opened up. Putting the phone in her blouse, the only place that she could think to put it and closed her eyes against the flashlight that was being used. She didn't know what she was going to do but she hoped that she could get a message to Ewing like this. If they caught her with the phone, they'd surely kill her.

"One of them is dead already. Didn't I tell you not to give them too much? Now we've lost out on about two grand. Fuckers. He might not even pay us at all if we don't do what he says." She nearly sobbed but didn't speak when she was jerked out of the trunk and tossed onto the ground. "He's going to be pissed off. We were told to get him three girls and now we're down to two. I'm not taking the shit for this either."

As the men were talking, she heard from her sister through their link. Liza nearly cried again when she spoke to her but Pauline told her to just try and act like she was still out.

"There were three of you in the car when you left for the mall. Do you know who the other two are?" She told her sister their names and that Devlin was brother to Tally, her friend. Liza told her about one of them being dead, but she couldn't tell who right now. But told her the names, as well as Devlin Hamilton, was the driver. "Good. His car is a piece of shit. Can you see the car enough to tell me if it's the same?"

"It's not." She lay there and looked around while the men were still talking to each other. "One of the guys is Vance Tetters, I believe. He works at the movie place. I swear, Pauline, I didn't do any drugs. They put something in me from a shot. I'm so scared that they're going to kill me, and I was so mean to Mom. Will you tell her how much I love her? Please?" She was told to be still as she was talking with the Cross men. "Are they gonna find us?"

"I hope so." That wasn't very nice but it was more than she deserved right now. Telling her not to tell her mom had Pauline telling her to be still again. "All right. Can you see the license plate of the car? If not that, then can you tell me what color the plates are?"

"Tennessee. I can't see the last numbers, but the first ones are 908. It's not the car we were picked up in." She liked being able to help her sister. If for no other reason than they'd find her body quicker. Liza didn't want to die, but she didn't want to be eaten by the other animals around the park while dead, either. "There are four men. I thought there were only three at first, then—" She told her not to tell her anything that she didn't need. Like there were four men but not to tell her that she thought there were three. "I'm afraid."

"I know you are, honey. We're doing..." When she stopped talking, it terrified her. "They have the scent of the car. Just stay put."

She didn't ask her where she was supposed to go, but she didn't move either. When the next body was pulled out of the truck, she could see that it was Devlin, the guy who had driven them to the mall. And he looked as if he was dying or dead. They had beaten his face in, and he looked like a deflated mask at Halloween.

"Listen to me. The Crosses are using dogs to find you. If you hear them barking, I want you to tell me immediately. All right?" She said she would. "Good. Now, I want you to tell me what you can see? Anything?"

"Nothing. I'm afraid to open my eyes for too long because they'll see me." Liza didn't want to cry, but she did tell her sister that she was going to die again. "I know it because I've been stupid thinking that because I was a cat, I couldn't be hurt. Now, because I never listened to you guys in telling me to pay attention to things around me, I'm going to die."

"Are you finished whining? If you do that again, I'm going to beat your ass when you get back here. You have a sleuth of bears, a pride of cougars, and a bunch of magical people looking for you. Now shut up that kind of talk." She told her she was sorry. "The magical begins are having trouble finding you because they say that you're lying on something or a large outcropping. Can you kind of move around so that they can pinpoint where you are?"

She moved just enough to gather the attention of the men. Just as she was telling her sister what was going on, she was hit in the face by one of the men. She thought that she wasn't out for all that long as they were still kicking her when she came too. Liza didn't hear the dogs barking, and that depressed her so much. She didn't want to die but at least hoped they'd have her body home. Then they found her cell phone when it fell out of her blouse. She knew that it was the end for her.

The first bit of pain from her body being beaten took her breath away. After that, she never felt another thing.

Chapter 2

Ewing watched the people in the emergency room. There were three families here that needed to be and several others that were here for support. He refused to think that they were here out of some morbid curiosity. It was going to be a difficult few months ahead after this, and he was glad that he had his kids with him for a quick hug or just someone to talk to.

"How many other kids have they found?" He looked at Mark from across the room. "I know you have contact with someone on the force. I just want to know that this is much bigger than what we were first made aware of."

"Ten more females and two more males. For the most part, they're like the kids that we have here now. Their bodies are so mutilated that it's going to be difficult to make any kind of identification.

As it stands right now, sixteen kids are missing, with just the two males that they've found already. So we still have several female teenagers missing if you count the ones that were brought in tonight." Mark started cursing, and he didn't blame him. His thoughts were that this couldn't be any more terrible. "Devlin was the oldest at seventeen. You remember him, don't you? He borrowed your car to take his driver's test. Libby Hamilton, his sister, is just a year younger than him. Then there is Pauline's sister, Liza Halloway. And Pearl Duncan, who turned sixteen on the tenth."

Liza was the child because she was just too young to have been killed like she had, and was the girl that he'd spoken to—was it only last night? Devlin had been beaten to death. His brain had been exposed from the treatment done to his face and head. Libby had been torn apart. They'd tied her small body between a tree and the car and then jerked it into pieces, tearing her into so many parts that he wondered if anyone would be able to recover her entirely.

Pearl, the youngest of the four kids, had been mutilated with what they discovered was a towing chain. It looked to them that they'd taken turns using it like a whip on the child until there was nothing much left of her to be able to say that she was a human, much less the pretty little redhead that she'd been. But it was Liza that had taken the most beating.

When they came upon her body first, it was all he could do to keep his belly intact. They'd cut her up into so many pieces to form the word 'bitch' that he knew for the rest of his life that he'd never forget her. And in her mouth, really just her jaws because her teeth, as well as her skin, were gone, there sat her cell phone. As if they knew that she'd been talking to one of them all along. It had been too late to save any of the teenagers, but almost as soon as he and his brothers were on site, they shifted into their beasts and took off after the men who had dared do this to a bunch of mall kids.

"Mr. Ewing, can you tell me what happened to my son? They won't tell us anything other than he's...he was only seventeen years old. And his sister just barely turned...What am I supposed to do now? They were all I had in this world." While holding onto Mr. Hamilton, he could feel his body shaking with his emotions. "They were just kids, and they tell me that we're going to have to bury them quickly as nothing can be done for them. Why? I ask you, why did they do this to my children?"

"I don't have an answer, Mr. Hamiliton. I wish I did but I'm sorry that I don't." He nodded and pulled away, his face pale and his hands shaking. "Why don't I get you a cup of water. You have to be strong for your family, Mr. Hamilton. They're going to need you in the—"

"I don't want to go on, young man. I just don't have it in me to go on." Holding him again while he guided him to one of the many chairs in the room, he sat with the elderly man until his wife could be found.

Ewing wanted to say that he knew the grief that they were going through. Losing someone to a senseless act, but he didn't really think that his losing his grandparents was anywhere near what losing a child was like. He wanted to scream for all the injustice in the world.

"Are they dead?" He looked at Mrs. Halloway, and he nodded. "Good. One less thing that I'd have to worry about. Did you know these monsters? Have you encountered them or their like before?"

"No, ma'am. But they were monsters." She nodded and looked at him again. He could see her falling apart. While her body looked strong and ready to take anything on, he could see the deep depression in her face that would linger there well after the men that had killed her daughter were nothing but dark soil in the woods. "Ms. Hamilton, if not for your daughter, we wouldn't have been able to bring any of them home. Not your child nor the ones that we found later. She was brave for what she did. Using her cell phone is more than likely what caused her death so quickly. Liza told her sister and me that she knew she was going to die, yet she was so brave."

"Pauline told me that she told her the same thing. That she didn't want to die, but that didn't stop her from helping out you fine agents. I'm going to miss her so much." She cried softly, and it hurt him deep into his soul. "She wasn't a good girl. Lippy when she had a mind to. Smart, but she never let herself shine. But she was my lippy brat, and I'm going to have a tough time going on without her there with me."

He held onto her hand while they sat there. Neither of them spoke but he did hand her tissues when she needed them. Looking around the large area, he was glad that Mark had suggested that they come here after finding the bodies and the men. There was no more they could do out in the field as they were all retired from the park, but it didn't bother them when the park's personnel asked them for assistance.

By midnight, he was about as exhausted as he'd ever been. Ewing still had to go home with the kids, get them into their beds, and then be up when they were up for the day. He knew that he'd have help in the way of the faeries, but right now, all he wanted to do was to sleep for about a thousand years, pushing out all the memories of the last twenty-four hours. He kept telling himself that his grannie would be proud of him and grandda would be patting him on the back like he'd invented children and their troubles.

"Mr. Cross?" He felt himself still looking around for his grandda when someone called him that. Mr. Ewing usually worked for most people, especially when they were pretty close in age, as he thought he and the woman standing in front of him was. "Are you all right?"

"I'd like to say yes, I have this, but I don't,

so no, I'm not all right. Are you?" She told him
that she'd had better. "What can I do for you?
Hopefully, it won't be too much, I'm dead on my
feet."

"I'm with the office of the president, and he
asked me to see you." Nodding, telling her that he
would do anything for the man. "He just needs
you to sign off on the paperwork for the upcoming
election campaign. I guess you're donating all the
wine for the event."

"Yes, I am. He told me about a thousand
bottles." He nearly fell into the woman. "I'm
suddenly not feeling very well. Could you help
me?"

He didn't know where she was leading
him, but he was glad when the two of them finally
stopped. Just as he was ready to beg her for a pillow
and a blanket, he was lying on one of the hospital
beds and being covered up. Telling the woman
that he had only a few minutes that he needed to
get to his children before he closed his eyes.

~*~

Trinity watched the man sleep. He didn't smell like
he was drunk. Nor did he smell like any drugs.
And she'd know that smell since her brothers were

doing it all the time. Moving the curl of hair that fell over his forehead, she thought that he had a handsome face, one that she could wake up to —

Stepping back from the man, she told herself that she didn't know what she'd been thinking. There was no way that he could be her mate, not for her. Leaning into his throat, she nearly came with the scent that hit her. Not only did it hit her nose but all of her senses seemed to have woken up as well. She'd found her mate.

Leaving the little room that he'd sort of fallen into, she found his brother, Mark. He'd been the one who had told her where to find Ewing. Now, all she wanted to do was to get on the next flight out and never return again.

"You look like you've had a fright. What's happened? Did you find Ewing?" She nodded, then shook her head. She'd found him all right but didn't want to. "Are you all right, Trinity? You're looking a little tense."

"He's asleep. He told me that he couldn't — he has kids?" She didn't know how that was possible if she was his mate. "How many?"

"Six at last count." Trinity felt her head swimming and had to hold onto something.

Reaching out to the door jamb, she looked up at Mark. He had six children? "They call him now when they have a stray child, and he takes them in."

"They're not his then?" Mark told her that he'd already adopted four of the children but was waiting on information for the other two. "He's married then?"

"No. He's not married. Just a wealthy single guy who takes in children when they need him. You didn't answer my question. Are you all right? You seem a little, I don't know, scary. Did he say something to you? I hope not. He's been on the go for the last...gosh, about two weeks now. What with the kids and the bodies tonight. He has a vineyard, too." She didn't want to be here but didn't know what to do either. "You're his mate. Aren't you? I mean, that's the only reason that I can figure out why you are worried about him having kids and not being married. Am I right?"

"Yes. He's a wealthy man, you said. I have...I have my own money. I can't be mated right now. You've no idea...well, you might have an idea what is going on, but I don't...I'm flustered." He told her that he could tell. "Don't make fun of me.

I'm trying my best here to not freak out. I have a job that I love, and he's going to expect me to drop everything and — I don't know if that's what he's doing to do, mind you, but my father did that to my mom. As soon as I was born, she had to stop her career, a good one too, and stay at home to be a mom. She never wanted that, and I don't either."

"Are you finished?" They both turned to the voice that was behind her. It was Ewing, her mate, and he looked about as pissed off as she'd ever seen anyone before. "I was tired and only needed a power nap. I'm going home." He looked at her. "You can go to hell."

As soon as he left, she felt the weight of what she'd said to him weighing on her heart. She'd been out of line and rude. She no more knew what he was going to do than she knew what she would do. Looking at Mark, she decided that he wasn't going to be too much help as he was looking at her with a cocked brow and a tight face.

She had to find him again and have him sign off on the paperwork that she'd been sent here to do. Now he was pissed off — with good reason, and she was going to lose her job because she'd pissed off the only man in the world that would have had her back if she needed it. Or she hoped that he would.

Finding him in the hallway near the elevators, she watched him with the little boy he had in his arms. He was a cutie, with chubby little cheeks and pink poised lips. When he smiled at her, just like that, she was in love with the little man. When he got into the elevator, she did as well.

"I need you to sign off on this, please?" He couldn't do it with the child in his arms, so he told her that she'd have to wait. "I can hold him for you."

"I don't want to get in the way of your career, Ms. Adamson." He handed her the baby and signed his name in the right places. When he started to take the baby back, she turned her back on him and glared. "Will you give me my child?"

"You're angry, and I'm sure he'll be able to feel it. I know that I can." As he shook himself of his anger, literally shaking his body, she took the opportunity to look at him. Christ, he was a great-looking man. "I'm sorry for my words. My assumptions. I've been working on my career for a long time and I don't want to have to give it up because of children. I never wanted any."

"Well, goody for you." He took the little boy, but not before she was able to give him a quick kiss on the cheek. "I'm going home. To my home. I didn't ask you, nor will I ever ask anyone to give up their lives simply because I thought that adopting the little people in my household was much more manageable than falling in love with a—what are you anyway?"

"Bear." Ewing told her that he got that part, but what did she do for a living. "Oh, I'm an attorney. I work for the president."

"So do I." When the doors opened on their own, he stepped out into the empty hallway and turned to her. If he were to slash her throat right now, it would be no more than she deserved. "Next time you want to make an assumption about someone, you should really take the time to watch them first. There is no telling what sort of information you might find out."

"Dad?" When he turned to the voices in the room behind him, Trinity could see that he had smiled. The little girl holding the door open was smiling up at Ewing. "Are we finally going home? I miss my bed."

The door clicked shut, and when she heard

the lock engage, she wanted to shift into her bear and tear it from its hinges and toss the man out on his ass. Like that would do her a bit of good, she thought. Pulling out her cell phone, she called her boss.

"I might have done something that is going to bite me in the ass." She said that Mark had told him that she was Ewing's mate. Then he congratulated her. "Ewing is the best of the Cross men. Loyal to a fault and a great man to have in your corner. I don't know that I'd be all that happy with you either if you were to talk about me behind my back. Are you on your way back here?"

"I can send the paperwork to you if you plan on firing me. In fact, I think I'd like that better than facing anyone right now." He asked her if she thought that he was a vindictive man. "No. But I know how much the Cross Bears mean to you. And I've royally pissed one of them off by being stupid."

"Mark told me that you were a bitch to his little brother. Also, outspoken, and you didn't have a single clue what you were dealing with, but, again, he said you were making stupid assumptions." She told him that she had. "Send the paperwork to me so that I can get that squared away and then you spend the next week fixing this with Ewing. I don't care if you declare that you love him from the highest mountains down there; I want this resolved in a week, or there will not be a job to come back to. You're right in saying that I'm fond of the Cross men. But what you did was uncalled for as well as something that I never expected out of you. Fix it."

The silence at the other end of the now-dead phone was deafening. She'd fucked up royally and didn't even know where to start on fixing things. He didn't say that she had to be a mate, but she did have to fix this thing with him.

After finding a place where she could not only fax the paperwork to the president, she also found an overnight courier service that would have the signed document in DC today. Girthing up her loins, as her father used to say, she went to find one of the family members to find out how to get in touch with Ewing. She had an idea that it was going to take more than an apology to make this right, but she'd do what she needed to do because her job meant everything to her.

Instead of finding one of the bears, she

found the mates to the others. Thinking that they'd understand where she was coming from, the five of them were especially cold to her when she said that she needed to find a way to contact Ewing.

"Why? So you can take a bit more of his heart out of him? He's a good man, and you made him hurt." She told who she thought was Jamie, Mark's mate that was what she was going to do, to fix this. "How do you propose to do that? From where I'm standing, and, correct me if I'm wrong, but you're only doing this to keep your job. Correct?"

"Yes, well, that's part of it. Did you have careers that you didn't want to leave when you met up with your other halves?" Each of them said that they didn't want to work anymore after finding one of the Cross men. "Well, good for you. I've been working for the president for the last few years, and I worked hard to get there, too. I'm not going to be giving it up without a fight either."

"It's doubtful to me that you'd have to put up any kind of fight. These men, though I guess you think that you already know them, aren't like other men. Nor shifters. When they tell you something, like they've got your back if you need them, then they won't step in until you say you do. As for working for the president, the eleven of us do as well." She wasn't getting anywhere with these women and told them so. "Good for us then. You'll be careful where you tread, my dear. There is no telling what will pop out at you in the best of times."

In the end, she had to call the president to get an address for the other man. Not only did she need that, but apparently, no one would give her a lift to his house, though they were all headed there now.

Stomping her feet to head out of the hospital she'd been sent here to be in, Trinity thought of all the things she was going to do with her free time without any children around nor a big handsome bear of a mate.

It took her eight hours to find a car to rent. It might have been less time but it only just occurred to her that she could rent a car rather than just assume that someone could take her back to the Cross homestead in their car. Sometimes, she never saw the trees for all the forests that were in her way.

Vowing to make sure that she kept records of everything that she'd had to do because a man got his feelings hurt was beyond measure to her. Stupid fucker. Turning up the stereo in the car, she knew that it wasn't to drown out her signing but to make her heart feel better about what she'd done. To a near stranger, no less.

It was nearly midnight when she pulled into town. You'd never know it by the way that the park entrance was busy, nor with all the restaurants' colorful signs lighting up the way so brightly either. It was as bad as Vegas, she thought, a town that she didn't care for any more than she did having to talk to Ewing again.

Finding a hotel proved to be just as difficult. It was high season, whatever the hell that meant, so all the hotels were full. Even finding one off the beaten path seemed to be something that was out of this realm of possibilities. She was about as pissed off as she could be when she was told that she should have made reservations. Again.

"I'm here on business." Well, she was sort of. "I need to find one of the Cross men in the morning then I'll be able to leave. I only need a room that has a shower and a clean change of clothing."

"We don't have clothing here. But there are plenty of places along the strip where you can get yourself a nice T-shirt and some shorts. If you're looking for any other attire, then I'm afraid that you're going to be out of luck." With a wink, she leaned into her face. "If I had me a chance to go see one of them Cross men, I'd wear very little and say less than that. The last one, Ewing? He's the best of the lot if you ask me. He's been taking care of those kids like he gave birth to them all on his own."

"He doesn't have any help with them?" She told her that once in a while, one of them would go to the house and let him take a shower, but mostly it was just him. "I'm to understand that he has a great deal of money too. Why doesn't he just find someone to live in with him?"

"Oh, he's not like that. Like his brothers, if they have a responsibility to someone or something, they go all out in taking care of it. I've never known a one of them that wouldn't stop. Even when they were rangers on their way to work, they'd stop and change a tire or something. And at Christmas time, they give away tons of toys for the drives and candy too." This didn't sound a bit like the man that she'd conjured up in her thoughts about him. In fact, it was the exact opposite. "They were devasted when their grandparents died.

The mister was killed in the line of duty. He was a volunteer here at the park and the missus, she simply couldn't live without him and passed on that very night. Sad story but true."

"Do you have a number for any of them? I don't want to just pop by to talk to Ewing." She asked her if she had lunch yet. "No. It's barely… well, I forgot about the time change. No, I've not had breakfast nor supper last night, now that I think about it."

"He's over at the diner. The one just about a block from here. The kids are with him, so he might be too busy to talk to you. He just loves those little kids." She asked for directions and was out the door before she remembered that she'd not had a shower yet either.

Oh well, the sooner she was able to get back to her perfect life, the better. She didn't want children, and she didn't need a mate. As soon as she walked into the diner, she knew that her perfect little apology to Ewing wasn't going to be so perfect after all.

There were police in the little place holding onto one of the children she'd seen with Ewing yesterday. The child, she couldn't have been any more than six or so, was screaming her bloody head off. The baby was crying, and Ewing was in the headlock of some very upset man. Going up behind the man who was holding Ewing, she jerked his arm around, freeing her mate. The police freed the little girl, and she came running to her. Not her dad but her. Picking her up, the little girl was a mess of tears. She asked Ewing what was going on. As calmly as he could, she could tell he told her that the man that was in the police custody said that he was going to take his prize back. He did that quote thing with his fingers so she had an idea that he didn't think that his daughter was going to be a prize to anyone.

"Mr. Anderson here said that he bought and paid for Patty, and he was either going to get his money back or take the child. I, of course, offered him his money back, but he told me that he'd changed his mind." Ewing let out a long breath before continuing. The baby was still crying, so he picked him up in his arms and snuggled him for a moment. "Patty isn't going with anyone. She's my daughter, and I told him that. But he said that if he didn't get one of them, then he was going to kill me and take them all, including Billy here."

"Are you pressing charges?" He just glared at her. "Look, buster, I didn't want to do this, but it was either, but I had to save your ass so I could get back to my job."

"Yes, I'm pressing charges. May I have my daughter back, please?" She sat down at the table where all the plates had been dumped on the floor and around the restaurant walls. Picking up some of the silverware, she smiled at the waitress when she came to the table. "What are you doing?"

"Can we have this cleaned up, please? Or better yet, I'll help you clean it up if I can get some food. I'm starving. Is there another place that we can have a seat?" The waitress told her that she had the mess and a table just for them. "Thank you so much. And I'll pay whatever it costs extra for this needing to be cleaned up, too."

"You go on with yourself now. I got this." Taking the hand of one of the little girls, actually she'd taken hers, Trinity made her way to the other table to have a seat. The other two girls and the car seat with the baby in it again were brought over by Ewing. Patty, the one who had been nearly kidnapped, was still crying, so she took her to the bathroom to get her cleaned up. The other two girls, she didn't know their names, came with her to keep a watch out for the bad man again. Somehow, the child had ended up with syrup all over her head.

"Dad won't ever take us out again after this. And we were being so good." The middle child, she was told her name was Harper rolled her eyes before continuing. "People just suck if you were to ask me about it. I think that I'll just live and die on the mountain and never come to town again."

"That doesn't sound so good." She told her that she didn't know the mountain. "True. I'm assuming that you live in a log cabin or something."

"Get real. We live in a big house with lots of stairs and bedrooms. Dad said that we have all that room, so we might as well enjoy it. We also have a pool, but it's not open right now. Dad's been waiting until we get swimming lessons before he'll do that."

The three little girls talked around her. They were polite and she only just realized that they weren't related. Not by blood, anyway. As she was getting Patty's hair pulled up into a messy bun, they were ready to go back to their food. So was she.

Chapter 3

Their breakfast was uneventful after the police took the man away. What he didn't understand was why Trinity was still here when she could have said whatever she wanted to and left. Finally, he'd had enough of her talking to his children.

"Why are you here?" She told him that she wanted some food. "There are about fifty restaurants around here that would love to sell you something to eat. So again, why are you here?"

"I have to apologize to you." She looked up at him from her sausage that she's speared. "I mean, I want to. I was told that I have to fix this, whatever I did to piss you off, but—"

"You owe a quarter to the cursing jar." She dug out the change purse from her purse and handed Patty the required quarter. "Sometimes I see Dad put a lot of money in the jar, and he goes outside for a while. I think he's out there cussing up a storm or something."

"What does the money go to?" Thinking that it was going to be some vacation or something equally extravagant. When she was told, it humbled her in so many ways. "That's a good idea. Using it to buy Christmas presents for—"

"Don't be nice to them. You want nothing to do with them." She looked around the table at the faces that, in the last few minutes, had come to mean a great deal to her. She could tell, too, that he was embarrassed by what he'd said. "What I meant to say was, you don't need to be nice to them. I accept your apology, and now you can go home."

"Just like that. You're going to let me off the hook for saying those nasty things to you." He told her that since he wasn't planning on seeing her again, that made it fine by him. For some reason that hurt worse than anything that she'd ever had hurt her before. "Look. You have a life. I get that. But I do as well. I love watching over the kids, loving them, and spending time with them. Could I use a break? Sure but that's not anything to do with you. It's my family, and I understand that it's too much for you."

She wanted to cry. Never in all her adult life had she wanted to have someone to look at her the way he did his children. Someone to care enough that she wasn't kidnapped. To be all right with chocolate syrup on their pancakes. Putting down her fork, she looked at him.

"You're right. I'm sure you hear that a great deal. I don't mean that to be mean, but you seem to be a man who has his head on straight. I'll leave you now." The girls, as one, told her not to leave. "Your father is correct. I don't want children, and I have a life that doesn't involve getting married. Thank you."

She was nearly to the door, thinking that she was going to make it to the street before her tears fell when someone, a very short someone, put their arms around her legs. Looking down at the little girl, her name was Beth, she had found out she asked her what she was doing.

"Don't leave us. Please?" She told Beth that she had to go back to work. "Nothing is more important than family. We're 'pose to be a family. You can't just leave us here with our dad. You have to be his wife, so we have a momma."

She was ready to bolt, thinking that there was no other way that she was going to be able to get out of this with her dignity or some semblance of it when Ewing was standing there. He asked her politely to please come back to the table with them. Nodding, she let the tears flow then, there was no hope for it.

"Don't cry, please?" He handed her a tissue and realized that it was used. "I'm going to buy stock in tissues when I get home. They're good for all kinds of things." Digging through his pockets, he found one that looked clean and handed it to her. "I think that the little packets of them are better. And softer, too."

She had no idea why that was suddenly funny to her. As she was wiping at her tears, she walked back to the table. The kids were still eating, but the smiles that were all around the table were worth every second of her pained heart. Trinity realized that she wanted this, the home life, more than she did anything. Looking at Ewing as he cut up pancakes into small blocks, she realized that at some point in her coming here and nearly leaving, she'd fallen in love with Ewing.

It was the way that their kind did things. Fast

and hard. But she was still leery about what to do with her life. She just couldn't be a full time mom and feel like she was making anything of her life. She kept thinking about her parents. They were forever bickering about the smallest little things.

"Do you 'pose they have whipped cream?" Trinity asked Rachel if she wanted some. "Nah, I was just wondering. They seem to gots everything else a body would want on pancakes." She had to agree with her. They did have a large selection of toppings for pancakes and waffles.

The conversation flowed nicely, even between her and Ewing. He'd answer one of the kids like he wasn't bothered by their constant questions and she did the same in turn. It wasn't until the waitress came by to ask about refills that she realized that the kids were sharing a single order of pancakes. It ticked her off a bit that he was taking advantage of the place by not paying for everyone an order.

"I think we're about finished here, Milly. Make sure you charge me for each of the kids. It couldn't have been easy waiting on all of us. But you did a wonderful job of it." He looked at her as if he knew what she'd been thinking. "I really wish that you'd start thinking positively of me instead of thinking that I'm taking advantage of people. Believe it or not, I'm not a bastard, nor am I cheap."

When he picked up Billy, telling the girls he was going to go and change the baby to not move, Trinity looked around the table at the little girls who had a large piece of her heart already. It was Harper, the most outspoken of the children, who asked her why she was being mean to their dad.

"I didn't realize that I had been." She said she had that mad look in her eyes. "I'll have to work on that then. I wanted to ask you if you would help me with that, but I'm afraid that you'll be too harsh on me, and it'll upset me."

"I won't be hard on you." She looked at her sister, sort of looking for support, she thought. "I'll help you because you are trying. Dad said that if you mess up on accident, that's all right. But don't do it again. Like when I spilled my milk because I didn't want him to help me. I learned that the jug is too big for my little arms, and I need help. He said asking for help is a good thing to learn."

"I know that's easier said than done, asking for help. You don't want people to think that you're some kind of wimp or something like that." She was going to have to keep watching her language. Ewing would never forgive her if he had to explain what the word pussy meant.

By the time Ewing returned with a much happier Billy, she'd paid the bill and tipped well. When he asked her, quietly how much she had tipped, she wasn't sure what he meant. But she did understand when he pulled out two one hundred dollar bills and put them on the table.

"For the other mess, too." She'd forgotten about that, having so much fun with the kids and Ewing was a nice distraction for all the bad things that were going on in her life. "You'll come with us, right?"

By the time they were outside, she couldn't believe how beautiful the day had gotten. Since the girls wanted to walk around a bit, she was willing to take their hands in hers to help out. Billy had a front carrier thing that Ewing was wearing, and Trinity laughed when Patty called it the Billy pouch. Apparently, Ewing was reading the Winnie the Pooh series, and they had learned about Kanga and her son.

There were plenty of shops on this end of town, but they were more centered on the townspeople rather than the touristy people. As soon as they entered the shop that had beautifully displayed items from the area, she thought she could spend her entire check in the store and not get everything that she wanted.

"We have this one in our house. The bathroom stuff is smelly, but in a good way. Dad brought us here when we first lived with him. To get us bathroom junk." She looked around and then motioned for Trinity to move closer to her. "That lady at the counter is trying to steal him away by telling him that she'd love to get to know us. Like someone wants to get to know us when there is a big handsome man around."

Against her will, she was falling in love more and more with Ewing's big family. When she decided that she was going to keep an eye on him, the girls seemed to be way ahead of her. They were dragging him all over the store to look at the displays and how much they wanted him to make their rooms look like this, too. Like they were really interested in a commode filled with pine cones.

"Help?" It startled her when she heard the word and looked around for the source, if there was one in here. After a few seconds, she had to ask who it was that was talking to her, and it turned out to be Ewing. "It's Ewing. This woman is going to abuse my body in the most sinful way if we don't leave here soon. Please, help by distracting her or something?"

Taking her cues from the girls, Trinity wrapped her arm around Ewing's waist while he was being shown the newest tea flavor in the store and smiled at him when he turned her way. Kissing him quickly on the mouth, something that she realized she needed more than her next heartbeat, she asked him if he wanted to have a cookout with the girls tonight.

He kissed her then and smiled. It was a devious sort of smile but she figured it was too late for her to back off now. Ewing looked at the girls.

"How about burgers on the grill tonight, my little ones? Hot dogs and brats." He looked at her again. "We'll have to go and get buns. There aren't any in the house that I know of."

"Good. I have the list from the house. We can get that taken care of, too." She had no idea what she was talking about but Trinity was certainly having a blast. When her jacket was tugged on, she turned and swept Rachel up in her arms and hugged her.

"Gee whiz, Ms. Trinity, you sure do give good hugs. Are you going to be our momma now?" She didn't answer because she'd gotten a good solid punch to her heart that made her slightly dizzy. However, what scared her the most was that she wasn't afraid to be their mom. It was, she realized what she'd been made for. To be a mom to these six kids and to help shape them into better human beings.

"Yes, I believe that I am." But when she turned to look at Ewing to get his take on her being the girls' mom, he looked at her like he was pissed. "I think I would enjoy that, but I can see that your dad might—"

Ewing took her hand into his and kissed the back of it. If it wasn't for the overly tight hold, she might have thought that he was all right as well. Wanting to jerk his hand from hers, she decided to fuck it all and get out while at least a part of her heart didn't belong to him when he started speaking to her.

"I can smell him." She started to look around. "No, don't. I don't want to alarm the kids but he's been following us around for most of the morning and yesterday. I didn't think much about it because he's a local. But it's him. The boss of the other four men that wanted the teenagers."

She'd heard about the death of the four teenagers and that they'd been mutilated beyond all recognition. Trinity didn't have all the facts, so she didn't know what Ewing was talking about with the man, but she gathered up the girls and went up to the counter.

It was much too close to the door, she realized when the man swept by her and it looked to her like he was reaching for Beth—she was the only one that she couldn't get between her and the counter. It was scary to think that he nearly got the child when all she did was reach out her hand to hold onto the children and wrapped them close to her while she paid for what she had picked out for the house that she'd never been to.

"Come on, girls. We're headed to home." She didn't want this man to know where they lived. More than that, she was terrified to think that he nearly got one of them. Once they were outside, her knees felt like they were going to buckle, but she held on until Ewing came out with her. "Are you ready?"

He shook his head before speaking. "I need to go into the hardware store for a couple of things. The girls are drawing us so many pictures that I want to hang them up in a way that we can display them all the time."

She wasn't sure she should follow him when he kissed her on the mouth again and asked her to go to the car. She didn't have one and had no idea where he'd parked, but nodded, telling him to be careful. Nodding, he left the seven of them standing there, including Billy, in his car seat and wondered what she'd do if something happened to Ewing.

~*~

Mac made his way back to the hardware store that he worked in. He'd damn near had himself a little girl. Or a passel of them. The people had been asking him if he could get them a kid to kill for weeks now, and it wasn't anything that he'd ever planned on doing. But they'd been right there. Five of the prettiest little things that he'd ever done did see. Then he'd tipped his hand somehow and lost out on it. Their momma she nearly snatched his hand away when he'd started to grab the one nearest to the door. Damned woman. He put out the open sign when he got the door unlocked.

He should have been the owner of the hardware place, too. But one of the Cross people had purchased the building right out from under him. Not that he could have afforded as much as they paid for it but he nearly had old man Mason ready to just hand it over to him for all his years of loyal service. Standing behind the counter when the door opened, he ducked down behind it when he saw two of the very Cross men that he hated with a passion.

"Mr. Mason around, Tetters?" That was another thing that he hated about the Cross men. They always used his last name instead of calling him by his first. "Tetters? Is Mr. Mason here? I wanted to see if the corks that I ordered have come in yet."

"There ain't been no deliveries in today, but he's already gone on home. His daughter picked him up about an hour ago." The nod. Like they knew he was lying to them. Which he was. "I know he ordered them. I saw him doing it." Another lie.

In a fit of rage about three months ago, he'd killed the Masons — and their little barking all-the-time dog when they sold this place to a Cross family when they knew that he'd been counting on it.

Also, since he didn't know the first thing about ordering and shit, there hadn't been anything ordered for the little shop since then, either. It did a fairly good business here but if he didn't figure out how to order more product, he was going to be selling next to nothing next month.

It was a good thing that he had his other gig going—which he needed to get with the boys that had been ordered to get him some girls for him to sell off soon. He needed at least that to be giving him cash money. He'd not have any money at all by the end of the day if not for that.

Everybody was paying by credit card and he couldn't get to that money as it went right into Mr. Mason's account every day. Fuckers. Who did shit like that anyway? Pay for things with a credit card all the time instead of having cash on them. Even the kids that he sold, nary a one of them had even enough to make a phone call. But they did have their cells, he thought. Damned—

"I'll have to go out to his home then." He asked him why he'd do something like that. "Because I need the corks he ordered for me. Why do you care if I go out there, Tetter? I mean, he's the one that I asked to order them for me. I would have thought that he'd have them in by now."

Mac decided that he was going to take one of the big eye hooks that he had on the counter and ram it into Ewing's face. Several times. With all his strength. The other one was some big deal with the Feds but Ewing had them pretty little girls. He was a fucking pussy.

What man would take little kids into his home—not even his own kids—without nary a person around to help with them. Christ, he just couldn't understand the Cross men at all. People were stupid to think that they were the smartest men on the planet. Also, he thought that women were just off their noodles, too, talking about how nice they were to everyone. Well, they'd never ever been nice to him.

He knew that they had money. A lot of it, too. But they never once offered any to him. Laughing a little to himself, he did admit to himself that he'd never asked for any money but they should have offered it to him all the same. Any fool could see that he was about as broken as the Masons were dead.

"I'll call him. I'm sure that he wouldn't care for you going all the way to his home to talk to him about corks, for Christ's sake." Ewing just looked at him, and Mac worried that he'd tipped his hand. So, letting out a long breath, he spoke to Ewing in a much calmer voice. "I'll call him and figure out what's going on. He put me in charge here, and I'd like him to, you know, think I can do a good job."

"All right." He thought that was settled, then the little fucker asked him if they had any of the other things that he'd ordered. "I believe that my brothers have some things coming in as well, don't they? It seems like things are taking longer to get to us now days. I wonder why that could be?"

"I don't have any idea. Might be because, you know that it's still the spring thaw or something. You know how nasty the roads can get when there is flooding everywhere." The asshole nodded like he had any idea how hard it was to get things in and out of this god-forsaken place. He wasn't a working man. "I'll gather up all the orders and call the places here in a bit. You just leave it to me. I might have ordered them wrong or something. I'll get on it."

"You said that Mr. Mason ordered them." He nodded, not sure what he'd said to the man but Ewing was nodding. "Yes. That's right. You told me that he'd ordered it, and now you're saying that you did. Which is it?"

Putting his hand on the largest of the eye hooks he'd been playing around with to use out in the old barn, he tried to think of the best way to get out of talking to this fucker. Just as he was going to pick up the hook and use it on him, the phone rang. Thank god.

The person on the other end was asking if they had any pen bolts. He knew what the person was talking about but hadn't been able to order them either. People would use them to build bear-proof fencing around their land to keep their animals safe. It didn't work, and just as he was going to tell the person on the phone that, the Cross's left him, and he simply fell to the floor and put his head on the front of the counter.

"Is Mr. Mason there. He knows what works better than you do, Tetter. Christ, for as long as you've been working there, you'd think that you'd have the first clue as to what all that shit in the store is for by now. Instead, all you do is walk around there looking like—" He hung up on the man. He didn't have time for that sort of shit either.

Pulling out his cell phone while still on the floor, he called the number that he had for Vance. It rang for a bit, and he was just thinking about what sort of message to leave when the phone was picked up. They answered it with 'Agent Farnworth, how may I help you' and confused him even more.

"I'm sorry. I must have dialed the wrong number." The man asked him what number he'd dialed. Before Mac could figure out that hanging up might be a better idea, he told him the number that he'd been given. "It's for a man by the name of Vance Tetters. No, that's not quite right. His momma was married, so I don't know… He's my nephew."

"Really? Then I hate to be the one to tell you this, sir, but Vance Tetters, as well as three other men, were killed not too long ago. I think that it's only been about three days now." He was glad that he was sitting down when he got that information. He wondered aloud what happened. "Well, they were doing something illegal, and it caught up with them. Are you, by any chance, their boss?

They had someone keeping them in line, I heard."

He closed the connection after thinking about who he was talking to. Were the Feds involved? Why did they care for his little business? Getting up, he pulled the closed sign down and locked the door to the shop. Getting on the computer, something else that he didn't know a great deal about, he logged into the local newspaper page, one that he'd been reading all his life, and found the article on the front page.

"Four men killed after killing four teenagers in a massive murdering spree." It went on to talk about how these four men had kidnapped three females and one male from the mall and had murdered them. In the most heinous way, the paper said. They'd been caught, it said, by the Feds and consequently killed. Then it asked if anyone had any news on the men or what they'd been up to because they had some other missing children that they'd like to put names to.

That meant that they'd found his dumping ground, too, he thought. Closing the computer when someone yanked on the door, he nearly laughed out loud when they tried three more times to gain entrance. When they finally gave up, looking in the window to see if they were kidding about being closed, Mac let out the long breath that he'd been holding.

It was just a little side business, he told himself. Why were the Feds involved? He could see the police being curious, but the Feds? It was just so that he'd have some cash, damn it. But it had also been really fun for him too. Like getting the girls ready to be sold off for the night had been his special treat.

Washing them down with the coldest water that he could have coming out of the tap at home, he'd then hang them from the rafters of the old barn on display. It had been something that he'd never dreamed of doing before. Not only that, but there were enough people out there willing to pay big bucks to fuck and kill someone smaller than them.

He didn't know how to make the computer work for him, so he'd just been making up flyers about having a man's night out had been simple enough. He had only meant to sell the girls to someone and then not have to worry about them being around. But the first man who won the bidding asked what he could do with the girl he was bidding on, and Mac had told him anything that he wanted.

The man bought and paid for the kid, walked right up to her, and put a bullet in her head. He was so shocked that it took him several minutes to understand that was all he wanted to do. To murder somebody. Then, he was asked how much he charged for disposal.

"It's not going to be cheap, you know. I have to clean up the place, then put them someplace nobody will find them." The man said that he was in a generous mood and would give him an extra five grand if he could do that once a month. So that was what he charged for just dumping the girls over a hill to let whatever was down there to have at them. Men, too, when they got smart with him. Though there weren't too many of those.

Since he had no overhead but the boys that worked for him, he was making a good profit off it. However, now that he'd been doing it a while, Mac knew that he was going to have to start putting some of the money to better use than just having a thick steak every meal and then buying himself all kinds of fun, manly toys like the new truck that was sitting outside in the parking lot.

He now had a boat, a pool, and even a pair of snow ski things that he loved more than the boat. The boat, a big one, had to be moored in the water too far away for him to get to use it every day, but the ski things? Why they were a hit with every snow fall.

Getting into his new truck, the sucker had everything that could be ordered on it, he made his way home. He had some thinking to do, and tonight wasn't going to be fun for him because it hurt his head to think. But he did feel better about getting home when he had his new baby.

The truck was bright red and had a pair of smoke pipes on it that would allow him to drive fast. However, with all the twists and turns around here, the highest speed that he'd been able to get to was fifty-five. And even that on long stretches wasn't all that easy. His plan was to have taken it all the way out to Vegas one of these days and race it up and down the strip. He'd heard of people doing that.

He'd not done anything to the Mason's house but move in. All their things, including the shirts that Mr. Mason wore all the time, were his to do with what he wanted. The freezer had been nice and full, and even it was beginning to look a little bare now that he had been eating all the stuff in it. The man had a great deal of bear meat and wondered if he could figure out where it had come from so that he could get more. There was even bison and elk meat, too. But he didn't particularly care for the elk meat. To him, it was just too gamey.

Setting up his meal to thaw out, he decided that tomorrow he'd go out to the dump place and see if there was anything around that might get him caught. He'd never taken any precautions always thinking that one of the bigger animals of the park would take care of the bodies for him.

Glad that he'd remembered to bring home the laptop, he decided that as soon as his supper was over, he was going to figure out this ordering thing. While that was going on, he was looking at all the newspapers that had been delivered to the Masons since he'd moved into their home. It wasn't like they were going to use it.

The Masons surely had to be gone by now, having been the first body that he'd dumped in his special place. Even the gun that he'd killed off the couple with was there. He was going to be in a lot of shit if he got caught. He was sort of happy to know that his nephew Vance was gone so that he didn't have to worry about him telling on him. Paying him a small part of what he'd been making had been little compared to what he'd get when the night was over.

Chapter 4

Ewing was glad when it was bedtime for the kids. He just needed to relax his mind a bit so that he could figure out this thing with Tetters. He knew that he was the man behind the kids being killed the other day. Knew it in his heart and soul. But what he was afraid of was that there was something more going on, and this was because he knew that Tetters was as dumb as a rock, so how did he figure out to kidnap the women?

Also, and this terrified him even more, was how was he selling them, to whom, and what did they do that had them ending up in a crevice on the mountain? He looked at Trinity when she said his name. He was sure that she'd said it more than the one time, too.

"I was thinking about Tetters, the man that looked like he was going to snatch up one of the girls." She said that she was sure that he had wanted them. "I didn't want to think about that, but you're right. And that makes me more uncomfortable when I think about what he was doing with the others that were killed." She told him that she didn't know what was going on with that.

"Oh, that's right. You weren't here when the girls were found to be kidnapped." After telling her what had happened that night, he went on to tell her of finding the stash of bodies. "There are ten so far that we can't put an identification to. The two men were easy enough to figure out. We'd only had the two missing and now they're accounted for. But since their bodies have been down there for some time, there is no telling what happened to them prior to them being dumped. Some of them have bullet holes in their bodies, others knife markings. It's hard to tell what the animals did to them versus what actually killed them. What we do know is that they were all dead before they ended up there."

"So you had these four pieces of shit kidnapping teenage girls, ten of them—" He told her that it was a total of twenty-three so far.

"Christ, that's a lot of deaths, but they were taken someplace that perhaps this Tetters person knows about, and they're killed."

"Yes. We know that they had a boss, too, the four pieces of shit, I mean. Someone that night they were to take the girls to. But one of them ended up dead before they got to their last place. Liza, one of the girls, was keeping in contact with her sister, and she told her that there was a boss that was going to be pissed off because one of them was dead. The only reason we have that information is because when they gave her the drugs to knock them out, they didn't count on her being a cougar shifter. Otherwise, there is no telling how long it might well have been before we could have found them. And a great deal more bodies piling up as well. If at all. Also, we've had a look around. There isn't anywhere that we can find where they would have stashed the kids so that Tetters could get them." She asked if he had a house or something that they could be stashed at. "I think, and this is something that my brother Mark said. He pointed out that Tetters is a lazy fuck and wouldn't be far from where they'd been killed to dump them. The land that he was dumping them in was in the park.

And that area is butted up to my land here. Like close enough that he could…he just recently got him a new truck. I saw it in the lot. So he's making money off of this. A great deal, too, if I don't miss my bet."

He thought of something else. Two of the elderly people who had been in the dumping ground had been unidentified. They'd been on the bottom of the pile of bones, and it was difficult to know who they might have been. Ewing thought for sure that they were the Masons. It would be like him to kill them off for no reason. He decided to reach out to his brothers and tell them what was going on.

"Why are you doing this right now?" It was his brother Gibb who had asked him. "Isn't your mate right there with you? You should be wooing her, not trying to solve crimes. I understand that this is important, but damn it, Ewing, she's right there in your house."

"What did you expect me to do? Huh? Throw her to the floor and have sex with her. I don't know if you know this or not, but I have a houseful of children who are still trying to get used to having a meal when they want it. All I need for them to do is walk in on us having sex on the floor." He told him that he'd watch the kids. "Thanks for that. I might take you up on that sometime, but right now, we're talking, and I don't care what it's about so long as we're together and not arguing about stuff. And this is important. I think that Tetters tried to take one of my daughters today. If not for the quick thinking of Trinity, I think he might have gotten out the door with one or more of them."

"Christ, you should have started with that. Are they all right? I can come over if they need their big uncle to care for them." He told Barron that they'd gone to bed without any idea how close they'd come to being taken from them. "I'm sorry, little brother. You tell us what you have, and we'll…can we come over? I mean, it's not that far, and I think that it would help. Hell, we'll even get some food to bring over."

In the end they did come over and brought their wives. They were sitting around the dining room table talking about everything pertaining to the case when the sun was just coming up. After making a couple of calls to the Feds about who he thought the elderly couple might have been brought them to his house as well.

He was never so happy to have a cook as he was right now. Even the women, who were usually so vocal about having a good meal, had been set to have donuts for breakfast after spending all night working. Milly, their faerie cook, was thrilled to be able to cook for so many. He was just happy that she didn't go running out of the house when she showed up to work today.

Everyone went home after helping with the clean-up. The mess they'd made not only in the dining room but the living room as well wasn't that difficult to clean up because of the magic that everyone seemed to have. Just before Amelia and Frazier left, she asked if she could use a little of her magic to find out where the bodies had been killed.

"I know that with the Feds involved that you have to be careful of how you find out the information. But I know the location now. Also, the people that have bought and paid for the chance to kill someone." He asked her if that was true that people were paying to kill people. "Yes."

She didn't say anymore and he was afraid to ask her for more information. She'd tell him, no doubt, but he wasn't really ready for it right now.

After she sat down, asking him to have a seat, he asked if Trinity needed to be there. Her smile told him it all. She needed to be involved, too.

Once they were seated, tea and crumpets showing up about the time that they were seated, and he and Trinity were holding hands. He was about as nervous as he'd ever been about anything in his life. Terrified as well. This was going to be epic but more like a hurricane rather than good news.

"He is the one in charge. Bert is." That was all he needed to hear before he could breathe easier. Knowing the enemy was nearly all the battle his grandda used to say. "How he did it was a miracle. The man is ten kinds of stupid. All he's done to advertise is hand draw an advertisement that says simply 'anything you want with teenagers. He has about twenty people show up, and they bid on the chance to have whatever kind of fun they want with some teenagers. He's figured out, through his nephew Vance, that girls were easier to catch as they were tiny and frail."

"They drugged them then take them in their car someplace, and that's where you know they've been...is it just murder or sex too?" She told him sometimes it was both. "Christ. So, how long do you suppose he's been doing this?"

"A few months. Right after he killed the Masons because they sold the store to you, he's been making a living on doing this murder spree with the girls." He didn't want to believe that he had anything to do with this and it was Trinity who told him that it wasn't his fault. "He isn't getting paid from the store. Doesn't know how to order things. He hasn't the first clue either about how to get on the internet and even look things up. He can read the paper online because it was logged in all the time when Mason worked there. I think that we're lucky in that he knows shit about the internet. If he'd understood even the basics, he would have more deaths on his head because he'd be getting them from more places instead of just locally."

"Locally?" She nodded and said nothing else. "This is by far worse than anything that I've ever encountered. I don't know what to do with the information that you have. Other than to go to bed and not ever wake up. I...I don't know what to do? Take a walk? Is it on the Mason's property?"

"No. Yours." That made him nearly sick.

These killings had been going on right under his nose for the last few — the slap to his face about knocked him off his chair. While he didn't understand why he'd been hit, he knew better than to retaliate. "It's not been going on under your nose. Yes, I read your mind. Buck up and figure this out. Otherwise, we're going to be sitting on information while the bastard is still out there causing the deaths of teenagers all over the fucking town."

"We should just tell them. Everything." Amelia asked Trinity how that would work. "I don't know. I really don't but sitting on it, that seems like we're just as guilty as Tetters is. Or...I just thought of this, tell the president. He knows what's going on here. We should see what he would want us to do with what we know now."

"I love that idea. He could say something like he had some pictures come back that had what...no, that won't work. Perhaps he could say that it was an anonymous caller...nope won't work either. They'd have to be cleared through the system before talking to him, and they'd not have his private number." Amelia smiled when he had a sudden thought. He didn't want to think that she planted it there for him to figure out, but he wasn't going to ask her.

"I was thinking that I should have one of the officers say that they've seen something suspicious and checked it out and saw what looked to him like a crime scene. Surely, there will be blood everywhere. And if not, then I can use some of my mojo to make sure that they can think there is." She winked at him. "You're very good at keeping your mouth shut when you need to. Aren't you?

"Yes, that's it. And I'm not stupid enough to think that I have all the answers." He loved this idea and when Amelia told him that it was taken care of, he believed her. Now, they had to catch Tetters so that this sort of thing didn't happen again. "He might leave town in his big new truck. How do you suppose we can keep that from happening?"

"He won't be able to leave the house." He didn't ask. As much as he wanted to know, he didn't want to know either. "Also, he's going to have trouble with his truck that makes it so that it won't run well."

If it was fixed by Amelia, he had to believe that she had covered their asses as well. Something like this would make national, hell, even worldwide news and he didn't want to bring his kids into this. Not now that they were beginning to trust people around them. And he had no doubt that it was going to be a shit show.

Getting the kids going this morning was fun. The three youngest of them had been going to preschool to see where their education needed to be. Their studies were sorely lacking, but they were catching up. The two older girls were going to second grade to see what sort of education they were missing. He knew that Patty could read, but not Lily. They'd been working on that nightly since she came to him.

Today was the first time since they'd been staying with him that he got them off on time. It had a great deal to do with having a second pair of hands. Trinity had even been able to fix their hair for them so that it wasn't just brushed but put into a nice braid that he'd not been able to manage, no matter how many videos he watched.

Billy had his second bottle by the time he was able to make it out to the vineyard. He was a little nervous about leaving the little man with Trinity, but she assured him that she was going to enjoy it. Besides, she had the faeries there so that if she needed anything, they could help her take care of it. She was also going to figure out her job situation with the president so that she could go back and forth to work while he stayed with the kids. If that was something that she wanted to do, she told him before he left.

"I love the kids. As much as I think they like me." He assured he that if they didn't like her, they'd tell her. "Oh, good. I think. Anyway, I can work from home most of the time, but I would have to go to DC a few times as well. I don't know how often but I know that my job depends on me being able to interact with the president personally at times."

"I don't even know what it is you do for him." She told him that she was his go to person when he had to have a talk with one of the people in his office as well as dinners and such. So he'd not say or do the wrong thing that would get him into hot water over it. "That sounds like a good job. Does he mess up much?"

"Not as much as he used to before I came along. Believe it or not, he would just say things that are now considered to be taboo nowadays. Saying the wrong nationality or even calling someone of color by the wrong culture could and would get him into trouble with entire nations. Also, I'm an attorney."

"That's wonderful. I have a vineyard — which is where I'm headed after I take the girls to school. The vineyard is one that I make most of my money with. Actually, I have several of them and sell my wine all over the world." He laughed. "Not to brag, but it's been very profitable for us. There is an us now, right?"

"Yes, I'd like that." She shyly put out her hand, and he took it. Holding it next to his cheek, he inhaled deeply of her scent. "I know that you guys have this thing about it's my body, and I should decide when we have children, but if it's all the same to you, I'd like to hold off on that for a while. Having six kids under the age of nine is a bit much for anyone, I would think."

He still, even a couple of hours later, was laughing about her telling him about waiting on having kids. He would have given her whatever she wanted, but was glad that she felt the way that he did.

The vines were coming along nicely. He was impressed and told them so that the faeries were doing just what he'd asked them to do. The new grapes were looking good and full, and when he walked into the winery, he was impressed with how much cleaner, not that it was ever dirty but it looked shiny, like a new penny to him. Perhaps it was because he'd not been there in a while, but he loved the look. He looked into the cork situation.

"We can make those for you, my lord." He wished they'd just call him Ewing but that wasn't going to happen, he didn't think. "I have heard that there is some trouble with them being ordered. It would only be enough for you to fill what wines you have going out soon. That way, we will not contribute to the downfall of the world."

"The world? But it would hurt the middleman in this case. However, I just discovered that the man is dead, so I might have to find someone else to get them for me. I could have gotten them cheaper by going to markets myself, but I like using the local people for that sort of thing. It's a nice income for them." She told him that she knew Ms. Mason and that she would grow the most beautiful flowers in the summer months. "You know you can plant some flowers around the vines if you wish. So long as they don't interrupt the grape harvest, you can use the land that is between the grapes."

"That would be most helpful, my lord." After showing them where they could use the soil, he was happy with the quickness of them getting them planted and started growing. It would be great if the flowers were to bring in more bees to the place. Pollination is critical for the grapes that he grew. Most anything, he knew.

~*~

Mac saw the cruisers go by the house three times. Well, that was all he noticed before it occurred to him that they might be looking for him. After giving them information about him being related to his nephew, he was sure that they were going to question him about his whereabouts concerning what he'd been caught doing. He had been practicing what he'd say to them all day yesterday and into the morning hours.

"I'm just going to blame it on him." He wasn't sure how that plan was going to work, but that's the only one that he'd thought of that would get him out of the picture, so to speak. "It's not like he can dispute my words over his. He's dead."

Looking at his phone when it rang, he decided that he was going to get out of the killing business for a while, too. It was too much to juggle the police, the men calling him to get his act together and get him another group to go after teenagers. His mind kept going back to the little girls. Damn, but they would have been a nice addition to his money maker.

When his phone rang again with the same number, he decided that he was going to get going on his blaming Vance for all the murders. Of course, he figured out that he couldn't say that it was murder, but he could, for now, at least pretend to know nothing about the boy's activities when he wasn't living with him. His mother would be rolling in her grave if she were dead. That was a sore spot for him.

Gertrude had been roaming the world since she'd been divorced from her husband. Not that he liked the other man, but his sister had made out very well when they divorced, taking more than half his estate and holdings. She was usually on a cruise ship, traveling around the world and would never, no matter how many times he asked her to send him any money. He knew that she had it, but she wouldn't share it with him.

Picking up the phone, he was surprised that

the call was so clear. It was his sister, Gertrude, who was asking about how much truth there was about her son dying. He told her what the papers had said about him.

"And you never thought that I'd like to know about my own son's death, did you? You bastard. I loathe you. I always have." He said that he didn't think she'd care all that much since she'd not seen him in decades. "I saw him just a month ago. We had a nice visit, and he even took one leg of the cruise with me. How dare you think that I'd not be devastated by the death of my only child. And to have to find out from my ex-husband, to boot. I could just strangle you, Mac. What is wrong with you?"

"Nothing. I mean, he's dead. It's not like he was anything to me. My nephew, of course, but we weren't close." He thought that was a brilliant thing to say in the event that his phone was being bugged. "I don't even remember the last time I saw him, as a matter of fact."

"Liar. You and he were up to something. Vance told me that you were making good money, he didn't say illegally, but knowing you, there is no other way that you could be. You're a lazy fat fuck now, just like you've been all your life." He looked around the room to see if anyone was in there to overhear what she was saying to him. "I'm coming home. And my home had better be in good shape, too, or I'm going to sue you for it. I'm sick of traveling anyway, so prepare yourself by moving out."

"I don't live there no more anyway." He thought of the state of the house and decided that it would be a good thing to blame on the kid, too. "Vance was living there for the last few months. I haven't been there, but—"

"Why must you lie all the time? I know that Vance wasn't living there. He told me that you made a whole mess of the place and had moved out a week or so before I saw him. I was just seeing if you'd blame him for it. You really are a bastard, aren't you?" He wanted to hang up on her, but she said she was coming home, and he wanted to make sure he was out of town when she got here. "Besides that, he's very neat, unlike you, so I know that if there is a mess, then you're the one who did it. Where are you staying anyway?"

"The Mason's house." Closing his eyes at the stupidity of his answer and now they'd know that he'd been here staying, he tried to backtrack. "They're out of town, and I'm house-sitting for them. They really are out of town, Gerty. I swear it."

"I don't care where they are, you old fool. Not that I believe you. You will always lie even if the truth is right there in front of you." She huffed at him once again. "I'm catching the next flight home, and you'd better be making the house look like I left it. Why I allowed you to move in while I was away...I must have had a brain fart or something. I'll see you in a few days."

With that scary parting, she simply hung up the phone. Jesus, that was all he needed now was his sister being around him all the time. Maybe he thought he could get someone to kill her off for fun. He'd almost pay good money for that to happen.

The second time his phone rang, the caller ID said that it was a private number. He usually would answer those but not today. He was too nervous after talking to his sister to try and keep his stories straight. He needed to write things down is what he needed to do and he was going to start that now.

By the time he was ready to cook his

meal, his phone had rang four more times. The house phone—who had one of those these days, he thought with a grin—had rang quite a few times, too. One of the calls was from the Mason's daughter. She was wondering why she'd not heard from them again. Now, he had to come up with another excuse as to why they weren't able to come to the phone. Putting his head down on the table, he decided that there was just too much going on for him to keep track of. He would almost go to the police to tell them what he'd been up to if not for the fact that he'd go to prison.

Answering his cell phone, he was nearly ready to toss it across the room, too. He realized how short he'd been when the caller asked him if he was all right.

"Yes, yes, I'm fine. Too much going on right now. Who is this?" He told him that it was Ewing Cross. "Oh good lord, what is it you want now? I'm sorting out things that are in the way, and I don't have time for you and your cokes."

"It's corks, not cokes. And that's the reason that I called you." He said that he called the place this morning and they'd not called him back as yet. "That's all right. Tell them I'm getting a refund from you, and that will be the end of it."

"From me? Why do I have to give you a refund if you didn't even get the corks yet? That's just stupid on your part if you think that I'm going to—how much are you talking anyway?" He told him. "For corks? That much for a couple of corks? Good god, what are they made of anyway? Gold?"

"They're made of corks, you imbecile, and it's not a couple of corks. It's three hundred thousand of them. The last time I got them ordered, they came here on a semi." He couldn't imagine that what he was saying was true. What the hell was he going to do with that many corks anyway? He remembered using the corks that had been in the brewery his parents worked at and using them to go fish— "Are you listening to me? I said that I'd be there first thing in the morning, so you'd better have my money. I know for a fact that they don't charge you for them until they shipped and since they've not arrived on time, I'm assuming that you didn't order them. So I want my money back."

"You're just causing me all kinds of trouble right now, and I don't like it. I have a great deal on my mind and—Well, I'll just tell you. My sister is coming home. She's not going to be happy with me—with Vance because he left her home in a wreck. She's also mad because I never told her that he was dead. Why would she even care, I ask you? It's not like he lingered around being sick before he kicked the bucket. Someone killed him, and I don't know what happened to his body even. Then there is the trouble with my money maker that I can't do because Vance put me in a world of hurt by getting caught and killed." On some level, he knew that he was saying too much, but he was on a roll and it was actually making him feel better to vent like this. "The police keep going by the house here. And the Mason's freezer is about empty. What am I going to do about food when that happens now that I don't have my money maker. I don't know, do you? Then there is the stupid store. I can't steal any money from it because no one pays in cash. Even for a little two dollar thing, they whip out that credit card like they don't have two bucks on them. Christ, I wish that I'd never started this shit. But it was a good—"

In that very moment, he realized all the things that he'd been saying and shouldn't been. He didn't know if he should hang up or not and was startled when Ewing started laughing. Asking him what he thought was so funny didn't help his nerves at all, either.

"You are. Christ, this is wonderful. I thought that I could distract you for a minute or two while the police surrounded your house or the Mason's home, but you just confessed to a great many things that I didn't care about while sprinkling in there the fact that you've been in business with your nephew as well as living in the Mason's home. We know that you killed them. You got your DNA all over their bodies. Also, and speaking to you just now, I'm not the least bit surprised to know how you managed to get an entire handprint of your right hand — in their blood, no less — on their bodies. Did you what? Hope for someone to catch you? It certainly seems like it." He let out a laugh, one that was enough that had him realizing that Ewing didn't think he was funny at all. "And if you ever come near my family again with the intention of taking one of them, I will shift into my bear and tear you apart while you're still breathing. Do I make myself clear?" He nodded, not thinking about the fact that he couldn't be seen. "You have a nice day, Tetters."

The police came into the house from the

windows and doors. There was nothing safe from the damage that they seemed to be wanting to create. They were dressed like he was some sort of drug dealer and might have some kind of army behind him. Even when they had him down on the floor, cuffing him and telling him his rights, he could hear Ewing laughing. What he could find so funny was beyond him, but there he was, laughing his ass off.

"Well, Tetters. Do you have anything to say about all this?" He said that he wanted his sister. "She's not going to be able to help you if she even wanted to. I don't think she likes you all that much. She's the one that called us saying that you had led her son down a merry path, and that was why he was dead."

He hated family. Especially his own and the Cross fuckers. All of them were a bunch of cock sucking bastards that were only out for themselves. At least he was honest about what he wanted and how he'd done it. He was out for himself, and everyone knew it. But family was sneaky. They'd get you in the back while they were hugging the stuffing out of you in the front. Or something like that.

Chapter 5

Trinity was having a good time with little Billy. He wasn't all that responsive about her talking to him, and he slept a great deal, but he was a beautiful child, and when he made a noise, cooing her mother would have called it, he seemed as startled by the noise as she had been. And he had the most beautiful smile that she'd ever seen.

It took her four new diapers before she gave up and asked one of the faeries to show her how to do it. However, they only snapped their fingers, and not only was he cleaned up, but a fresh diaper was on his bottom, and the snaps on his sleeper, which she knew was going to cause her nightmares, were fixed. She thought that a great trick but it didn't help her in figuring out how to put one on him.

"The instructions are on the box. I know that

Lord Ewing had to refer to it several times when he was getting used to changing the little boy. He's so beautiful, don't you believe so?" She told Mae, one of the many nursery faeries, that she thought he was the best-looking baby in the world. "I believe you might be right."

Mae told her that there were all kinds of things in the baby's room that she didn't understand. For the next twenty minutes, she showed her, after looking it up, what things were used for all the big and little things that were in the room. Trinity was surprised that Mae didn't understand the mobile on the crib.

Once she wound it up and the music began to play, the little bees, five of them in bright colors, began their dance around the base. Mae was so in love with it that she said she was going to have one over her bed as well. Trinity was surprised to find out that the faeries that worked in the house lived there as well. Also, those who didn't live and work there had homes of their own as well.

When Billy woke from his nap, she watched him stretch. It was the most amazing thing to see him crunch up like he did and then stretch out like he was a large cat or something that needed to make his muscles move around. Kissing him after picking him up, she knew that when he got older, he'd not like that as much. But for now, she was going to get anything and everything she could from him.

After he started getting cranky and needed another diaper change, she snuggled him up in his bed and watched as he fell asleep after his bottle. She wondered if he was getting enough to eat when he'd just doze off like he did. She decided to go to the office and look up on the computer about infants and their habits. Trinity thought that she should have done that earlier than after being here for a week.

She was startled out of her thoughts when Amelia showed up. "Don't move." She nodded and then asked if the baby was all right. "Yes, the faeries will watch over him. But I want you to stay right here until I tell you to move. To be honest, I don't know exactly what is going on."

Barely getting her first nod out, Amelia was gone. Trinity wanted desperately to go and check on Billy, he was all she could think about when Amelia returned. She asked if she could move, and when given the ok, she went to the office where his crib was and picked him up.

"I'd like to be mad at you for not explaining, but I'm afraid of you." Amelia told her that normally she should be, but not today. "What's going on?"

"Vance's mother is out on the warpath. She had some information that she wanted Ewing to clear up for her. It was his name and the fact that he was a park ranger that had her coming here." She asked why that had anything to do with her. "Nothing. But I didn't know that when I came to you. She's coming here because her brother told her that you and your husband, Ewing have been the ones that were blaming all this on her son. She thinks that you have it all wrong and came here to have you change your mind. Or she was going to change it for you. But I told her that she should be talking to her brother. That so far as anyone could tell, he was a person of interest in the murders that Vance seemed to have been involved in."

"Oh. She couldn't get in, you told me." She said that it didn't matter that she couldn't get in but that she'd frighten the household, which would include the baby. And that would have caused her to die at her front door. "The faeries, you mean.

They'd kill her."

"Yes. Without a second thought as to what kind of trouble she was causing, they would see her as a threat, and that would be the end of her." She didn't see a problem with that if she was a threat, but Amelia would know best. "While I'm here, I would like to get a bit of your blood so that I can trace you if necessary. I have all the children's, including Billy, but not yours. Not to say that I couldn't find you if I needed to, but it would be easier if I could just simply go there and get you wherever you are."

"All right. Is that the popping thing that Ewing was telling me about? He can do that, but I've not tried." She said that she should try it and that it was exactly what she meant. "I don't mind that at all. I should have a bit of the other's blood as well. Us being bears, it would be a simple thing for me to be able to locate them as well. Not to mention talk to the others when I need to. As it is right now, because we're mates, the only person that I can speak to is Ewing."

"Good." She put out her hand and with a sweep of Amelia's hand, it was done. "I don't really need your blood, but I do need a direct connection to you but most importantly, I needed your permission. We've touched before but I've never asked you if I can have the connection. It's all about granting me the usage with my magic and balance. So? What are your plans for the day?"

"I'm going to go and get the kids when they're out of school if Ewing isn't back. He told me that the faeries had done a great job with what they were tasked to do, and he's quite happy." Amelia told her that they'd be devastated if they had heard otherwise. "I can see that. They seem to have very fragile emotions when it comes to compliments or bad news."

"Yes. Mother told me once that it's because they are so competitive. You have to admit that there are a great many of them and it would be hard to be able to find one that does a great job at something. Most of them do, anyway, do a great job, I mean. But they also like to please, so if they're tasked with a job that has them picking up stones for whatever reason, they'll pick until they nearly die from not resting or having anything to eat or drink. That's why when you ask them for something, it's best to make sure that you give them a limit on whatever it is. Also, a time frame.

Measurements are a big help for them as well."
She said that she noticed that the little shed that
she wanted wasn't little. "I'm betting that it had all
kinds of magic as well. Like if you need something
that's not in it, you only need to close the door and
wish for it and it'll be there. Yes, measurements
are a huge help. Not always, but they do like to
please."

They decided to take Billy outdoors for a
bit of sunshine. Trinity was still nervous, but right
now, she was enjoying her time with her sister-in-
law. She supposed they weren't really related that
way, but she knew that each of them considered
the other to be a sister of their hearts because they
were all that close.

The warm sun was lovely. Being able to see
the other faeries at work, the flower faeries was
amazing as well. If you looked hard enough, you
could see thousands of them working and getting
so much done. The flowers in their yard were
beautiful because the little people loved the colors
so much. Trinity had a good time just wandering
around the yard and having a long conversation
with Amelia.

Amelia was the only child of the Grand

Witch. Actually, Amelia was the Grand Witch because her mother tricked her into taking the job from her. It was good timing, she'd been told that if she'd not taken the magic by then, Frazier and two of his brothers would have died. It was when a couple men, who died as well, blew up a mountain to get to whatever might have been inside of it.

"You remind me so much of Grannie. You're very calm and don't seem to have a lot going on in your head at any given moment. I have noticed that instead of thinking through the way a plan that you have for yourself, you think up and toss them out without requiring an answer from anyone. That's wonderful." She told Amelia that she wished that she'd had a chance to know the elderly couple. "You can ask anyone that lives around here, including most of the storefront owners, and they'll have a story to tell you. How she helped them with their homework when they'd gotten behind. Baby sat their children so that a couple could have a few hours to themselves. She was great at steering people into a better place without actually telling them that was what she was about. Grandda was like that, too, but he was much less vocal about it. But boy, oh boy, did they love one another. You could feel it from them by just being in the same room with them."

"I've heard that they had a love of the century. Do you think that you love Frazier the way that they did?" Amelia blushed and said that she loved him more. "That's so wonderful. I love Ewing."

It was the first time she'd said it to someone else. That she did indeed love Ewing. He was her first thought in the morning when she opened her eyes and her last thought at bedtime when she closed them. And throughout the day, she'd think of him and get chills from just that. A single thought. His scent that would linger through a room that he only just left. He was her everything. Life, breath, and soul. She truly did love him.

"You're thinking about him. I can see how surprised you are about something." She told her that she had never felt like that before. "And you never will again. This kind of love, it's the forever kind. And I do mean forever, by the way. I'm going to go with you to pick up the girls. Then they'll be better about coming to my house when they see you and not just me picking them up."

"You don't have to do that." She told her

that she and Ewing needed this time alone, and they had to bond, too. "I know that it'll make me stronger, but right now, all I can think about is it feels like I'm dumping five kids on you so I can get laid."

Amelia laughed. "Six kids. I'm going to take Billy too. He'll be no problem if that was what you were going to say. I have ten faeries to your one in my house. Not to mention, I have a great deal of magic, too, that I can use. We'll take the kids to my house. You go home after that and get yourself in a sexy mood and jump Ewing's bones as soon as he comes into the door."

She took her up on her offer. After explaining how she didn't need an overnight bag from any of the girls, Amelia did take the stuffed animals that were on each of their beds. Billy didn't need anything either, as Amelia was going to have fun giving him whatever he needed. Trinity was sure that all the kids would come back with much more than the things that they left with. And she found that she didn't care one bit either. If anyone needed to be spoiled a little, it was her children.

Picking up the girls, they were vocally excited to be going to Aunt Amelia and Uncle

Frazier's home for the night. They asked if they could watch a movie, and Amelia told them that she had the best ideas for them and that she wanted to surprise them with it. Whatever it was, she was sure that the girls would not just tell her all about it but that they'd both her and Ewing hear about it for weeks on end. And again, she didn't care.

After dropping off the kids with the other couple, she made her way home. She'd been told several times that the house was safe now and that no one could harm her or anyone inside the property. Just as she was getting out of the car, she saw the man standing at her front door. There was a bright white and brown pony near his side.

She'd heard that there were tribes all over the place in the mountains. For the most part they didn't interact with the tourists nor with the people that lived in the area. To have one so finely dressed and standing tall, she wondered how anyone could ever think that they were a bad sort of people for living like they did. So it surprised her even more that he was at their home.

"My name is Shaking Tree." She told him her name. "Yes, I have been told about you. No disrespect, but I was looking for your mate, Ewing

Cross." She told him where he was and what he was doing. "Ah, yes. I should have looked there first, but then I'd not met you."

"Thank you. Is there anything that I can help you with?" He smiled at her, and she smiled back. "I'm sure that there are a great many things that you could help me with, isn't there?"

"Yes, Red Fall. But you are learning quickly. And you are being a great mother to those lost souls in your household." She didn't know why he called her that, but she loved it. She asked him what it meant. "It means that your hair is the color of the red in the forests in the fall. It is a very true color that all trees strive to have. A true redhead that many will envy. The reason that I look for your husband is because I am the one that has found the place where the deaths of so many have occurred."

It took her a moment to figure that out, and when she did, she asked him if he was all right with being the one. His nod and stance told her that not only was he happy to be doing it, but he was very proud of the fact that he'd been asked.

"The Rangers, they know me and will be glad that the finding the place of so much death is finished. Once they come to the site where the others were murdered needlessly, many families will have closure, and that's a good thing. Also a great many families will have their family back with them." He bowed to her and then continued. "There will be great sorrow and celebration when this is a closed chapter in the Park."

"I agree." She reached out to Ewing to tell him who was here and what he wanted. "He wants you to be with him as it's your land."

"Our land, but I agree. It will keep me from finding out from someone else." Ewing said that he was on his way back now. "Good. The kids aren't here. They're all spending the night with Amelia and Frazier."

"Does that mean what I think it means?" She asked him if he thought he was getting laid, then yes, that is what it meant. "Hot damn. It's going to be a good time tonight. But damn it, I have this thing with Shaking Tree now."

"Well then, you had better hurry it along or ask one of your brothers to run point for you. It's not like they don't know as much as you do about what has been going on out there. Not that I guess you're to tell anyone what you actually know." He told her that he was going to get with his brothers and tell them to do what is needed. "I like that idea. I doubt very much you'll be missed with the others there."

She was still out on the porch when Ewing got home. Shaking Tree didn't wish to enter their home without the man of the house there. It was very hurtful until he explained to her that it was the way of his people. He was a good person and had a great sense of humor that she had enjoyed. She did not envy the task that he was going to be a part of. When Ewing was explaining that his brothers were going to go with him, Trinity went into the house. She wanted to get ready as quickly as she could for Ewing.

~*~

Ewing found Trinity in the dining room. She looked a little winded, and he asked her what was going on and if she was all right. At her heavy sigh, she explained to him why she was breathless and looked a fright.

"I was going to bring us up a fruit and veggie tray that I got on the way home and I completely forgot it in the car. And since I didn't want to interrupt your conversation with Shaking

Tree, I decided to make one up on my own." He smiled and leaned against the door jamb while she continued. "When I got to the kitchen, running from our bedroom to here, I realized that I didn't know where any platters were. So started rummaging through the cabinets in the kitchen when I realized they'd be in here. Finding them still was difficult as the faeries, bless their little hearts, decided to use magic to store things and made the platters small so they could get more things into the cabinets. While a great idea, it didn't help me any that I have no idea how to make them normal sized." She stomped her foot. "And now the mood is ruined because I look like a mad woman racing around the house for some platter food that I doubt very much we even eat."

"Let me show you something." He kissed the back of her hand and removed the dozen or so tiny platters from her hand. "You have to admit, they really are kind of cute." The low growl had him laughing. "All right. Here we go."

They were standing in front of the refrigerator when he opened it up. Just as she said, there were no platter food fixings. Really, there was nothing in the ice box, he called it, but a gallon jug of some brown liquid. He assumed it was tea but didn't want to take the chance of drinking something that he didn't know.

"All you need to do is close the door." He did that. "Then you just say what it is that you're looking for. Like cheese and fruit platter and meat and crackers platter."

When he opened the door, there were two platters of food in the space that had been empty before. One of them was filled with a beautiful arrangement of cheese and fruit. The other was filled with different types of crackers with an assortment of meats and sausages. She glared at him.

"You could have told me that before, you know. Also, it would have made me feel a good deal better today knowing that we're all immortal." He said, 'oops'. "Oops? That's all you have to say is, oops? I've been sick with worry all day, and it was all for nothing. I was afraid for you. Not to mention Billy when that crazy woman showed up here."

"Mae told me that we'd had a visitor. She said that Amelia got her all straightened out." Trinity growled again, and he laughed. "You have no idea how sexy that sounds to me. Like you're calling to my bear so that the two of them could mate as well."

"Maybe later. We can run through the woods and have a good time as our bears. But right now, all I can think about it having you inside of me and touching me. Any way that I can get you." He told her that she could too. "Ewing, everyone is going to know that Amelia is watching the kids so that we can get into each other...well into each other. Does that bother you just a little bit?"

"No. Because I know that my family will tease me, they never would you. Do they know that we're going to have copious amounts of sex—we are, right?" She nodded at him with a huge smile. "Good, while they know that, they also know that it's important that we bond and claim one another before anything happens. And while we are immortals, true immortals, we can still be hurt, and I don't want that for either of us. Hurting still has pain, and it would take some time to heal, so having you able to survive someone hurting you, they know that in order for us both to be stronger and live a better life, we simply need to bond."

He moved closer to her, putting the platters

back in the fridge. Putting his hands on either side of her cheeks, he gently tugged her next to him as he made love to her mouth with his own. And what an incredible mouth she had, too.

Ewing wanted her badly, but not here in the kitchen. He wanted her in a bed were he could touch her. Inhale her scent and claim her. There was plenty of room in this one, the counter, the butcher block in the middle of the room. Also, there were any number of places that he could take her on the floor or against the walls. Even the fridge, a large one for a household this size, could have held them both in a pinch. However, he didn't want their first time to be anywhere or on anything but the nice bed in their bedroom.

Pulling away from her, stepping back when she reached for him, he smiled at her and told her to go to their room. Trinity stared at him with her swollen, pouty lips. Her hair was a mussy mess. Slapping her once on her ass, the firmness of her muscles had him wanting to do more, but she got the idea and backed away from him. Everything in him wanted to give chase, to bring her to heel. To make her his.

Hearing her running up the stairs was

another hurdle that he had to make himself ignore. The thought of chasing her down again was forefront in his mind. Turning on his heel, thinking about anything else but his mate, he sent the lock home and checked on the other doors in the room.

No one could enter his home with ill will in their heart. But to him, there was no reason for him to be inviting trouble into his home. Locking the door, something that he didn't think anyone in his family did to this day, seemed like a no-brainer to her. Why have them on the doors if you weren't going to use them for what they were intended for? He made his way to the patio doors and locked them as well.

As he was headed to the front of the house, he heard from Mark. Being the king of all bears, he would know the precise moment that he and Trinity mated. It was the magic that he had as well as the others would feel it, too, because they were all related. Not every time they had sex, but this first time for sure. Instead of teasing him, something that he was sure he meant to do, he asked him about the land and the barn that the murders had been conducted in.

"It's going to be a while before you can use

the area. I'm not sure when the last time it was that you were out here, it's pretty dusty, but the Feds are saying that it could be up to a couple of years before anyone would be able to come within a mile of the place. They want to know if that's all right with you. However, I get the feeling that if it is or not, they're going to take as much time as they need to." He told him that's what he was figuring as well. "All right. They'll have manpower surrounding the area for the next few months. Just to make sure that no one messes with the crime scene. It's hitting the papers in the morning. Before I forget, none of us will be mentioned. Not even who owns the land other than the park area where the bodies were dumped. Anyway, people will be coming out here for weeks just to see if there is anything left that they can steal. Humans are odd, don't you think?"

"I've been saying that for decades. Just so you know, I think that there are a few dozen screws loose in some shifters that I can name as well." They both laughed and he relieved some of the tension that he had racing through his body just then. "Have them do whatever they need to do. To be honest with you, I had no idea there was a barn out there, much less use it. But once this is finished, I'll have it torn down and just let the land return to what it was before. Mountain tops and trees. How much longer are you guys going to be out there? Did they give you any ideas?"

"Few more hours. We'll be all right." Mark told him that he loved him, and Ewing told his brother that he loved him very much. "I'll see you tomorrow. We're still having a dinner to celebrate Grandda's and Grannie's anniversary, right?"

"Yes, I'm glad that you reminded me. I'll tell Trinity, too. Are there going to be kids there? I'd like to bring mine so they can hear all the memories that people had about them." He told him he'd better be bringing the kids. The women would have his head if he forgot them. "Trust me, Mark, one cannot forget that he has six children. No matter how hard they might try to forget them. Not even when there is only one with you. They'll remind you right away if you mess up, too. But I'd never do that. They mean the world to us and I don't know how I was living day to day without them around. Even Billy makes my day better just because he's my son. I wonder if it'll be any different if we have children of our body?"

"It won't for the two of you. You'll have those kids thinking that they were born to you two before too much longer. I have to tell you, Ewing, when you do something, you do it up right. I've never been more proud of any of my family than I am of you. I'm envious as well as terrified for you as well, just so you know that as well."

After closing the connection, he turned the lock on the front door. It was solid the two doors that were closed against the night but he liked to think that they were welcoming too. His grannie used to tell him there was no reason for a porch or a swing on it if you were never going to be out there to welcome visitors. And when Grannie was around, there were great warm hugs as well as happiness too. He made his way up the stairs and to his room.

Chapter 6

Trinity didn't know how to be sexy. Not once in her life had she been able to seduce anyone that she wanted to have a fling with. They usually told her that she was acting weird or something along those lines. Today wasn't a good day either, as she had no idea what sort of sex either of them liked. So, after using the bathroom, she met him in the bedroom, fully dressed. It was now or never, she told herself.

"Come here." She moved toward the bed, all the time thinking that she was finally going to bond with Ewing, that this would make them a couple 'till death they did part. "Come to me, love. I want to undress you in the worst sort of way. To see what treasures that you have for me."

She did as he asked, moving slowly toward him, fearful of tripping, which would be just like her, and falling on her ass. As soon as she was within touching distance, she reached out to touch his face, his cheeks, as well as the pounding pulse at his throat. Her body seemed to accept him as her mate, and she wanted him. He sat with her on the bed so that the two of them could touch. She was just happy that she didn't have to stand any longer. Her legs were weak with anticipation.

"I love you, Trinity." Ewing kissed her, making short work of not just her blouse but her bra as well. When she was topless, she leaned back on the bed so that he could remove her pants. Instead, he took one of her tight breasts into his mouth and sucked on it hard. Her fingers in his hair were nearly her undoing when he nipped at her nipple. Lifting his head from her, she watched him as he undid her pants for her.

"I've wanted you for so long. I cannot wait to see if your body is as beautiful as I have been thinking it is. Your breasts have surpassed my wildest expectations, full and tight. And your nipples are just perfect for me to suckle at. I need to know that the rest of you will as well."

"Hurry. I need to feel you touching me, Ewing." He took her pants off with her panties. He could only stare at what she was offering him. Not only was he the most beautiful creature that she'd ever seen, but her curls were dewy for him as well. She could feel her need running down from her pussy to the crack in her ass. She was so wet, she didn't know what to do with it all.

He told her that he wanted to taste her, and he got down on his knees in front of her after pulling her legs to the side of the big bed. Spreading her legs wider for him, she watched his face to see the emotions that were there. Want and need were fighting for control over him. She wanted him to touch her. But she also needed to touch him as badly. Her fingers shook as she thought of touching his cock and balls to see if they were as silky smooth as they looked.

Sliding his finger through the curls and into her, she moaned loudly and laid all the way back on the bed. Fucking her this way, him stretching and giving her as much pleasure as he could, she watched as Ewing reached down and pulled his own pants open. The cool air of the room nearly had her crying out. His cock was so painfully full seemed to call to her to take him into her mouth.

~*~

Moving his tongue through the wet lips of her nether region, he suckled on her clit until she cried out with her first climax. When she begged him to take her, Ewing did what he wanted since he'd sat down in front of her. He leaned into her pussy and fucked her none too gently with his tongue. Trinity screamed several times into a pillow that was near her. Pulling it up from the mattress to cover her mouth as she let go with the most primal roar that he'd ever heard coming from a female before. But she was his and would be forever.

Trinity squeezed his head so tightly with her legs, begging him to release her so that she could feel him inside of her. He wasn't ready for that. Ewing wanted to play with her. Tasting her like this, drinking down her nectar, he moaned every time she flooded his mouth with more. And there were copious amounts of her cream, so much so that it was dripping off the end of his chin and onto his chest.

Ewing fucked her, too, with his fingers. Stretching her pussy so that she'd not hurt when he took her. He knew he was larger than a human's cock would be. That was why he was being extra sensitive to her needs. He didn't want to cause her any discomfort the first time they made love. Nor at any time when the two of them were together.

"Ewing, please. I'm begging you to take me. I need to feel you inside of me more than I need to breathe." He sat up when she yanked his head up by his hair. Even his bear was afraid of her in that moment. "Fuck me."

He stood up, pulling his pants off the rest of the way. Not waiting for her to tense up again, Ewing filled her with his cock. He didn't know which of them had suffered more from the abrupted invasion, her or him.

His cock was strangled within her. Twisted up like it was, he couldn't move. As soon as her hips moved, adjusting herself, he guessed to take him, he moved too. It was both painful and pleasant at the same time.

Taking her mouth with his, he kissed her as he took her with his cock, body, and soul. Touching her body with his hands everywhere he could reach, he felt things that he'd never felt with a woman before. Each of her muscles and skin. Her breath as he nuzzled at her breasts.

Her ankles tightened around him when he lifted her ass up to meet his downward demands.

Each time she cried out for more, his body seemed to understand that she meant it and gave her what she wanted. His heart soared with love with each touch of his fingers, yet he was still careful. He didn't want her to be hurt after they were done.

"Give yourself to me." Her command was like a smack to his heart. He screamed out his own release, his bear doing the same when she bowed up from the bed, calling out his name over and over as she released. His back felt raw as she raked her fingers down over him, her nails digging deeply into his flesh. Blood, hot, raced down his back, and he could feel it gather in his spine.

When she came a second, then a third time, Ewing joined her. He came so many times that when he told her he couldn't move again, he was dizzy with it. Rolling to his back, taking her with him, Ewing moved so that he was still inside of her. Fucking her slowly so that her continued climaxes had a little more punch to them than she would have had without him.

Closing his eyes from the way the room swayed around, he held tightly to Trinity until he could see better. It helped that he knew better than to look with both eyes at the same time the second time as he was sick with the gentle movements of the bed. Just looking out one eye was enough to make him ill to his stomach.

When he woke up, feeling like he'd run a marathon of several hundred miles, Trinity's side of the bed was empty. Just as he was going to get up and find her, he heard the toilet flushing in the bathroom and waited for her. The room wasn't chilly, not by any means, but when she snuggled up next to him, her cooled body had him laughing at her.

"I debated for twenty minutes before I just couldn't take it anymore. I had to pee." She finally started to feel warmer, and he held her tightly. "You're so warm. Hold me."

He did, rubbing her back and shoulders until she began to relax. Closing his eyes, he started to fall asleep again then she spoke. Ewing could hear the tentativeness in her voice, and that made him smile. He didn't laugh. He wasn't that stupid.

"Is sex always going to be like that? Like it's the end of all of our sexual escapades, and we're the winners of the golden ring?" He did laugh then. She was so delightful that he didn't think that she understood what she was to him. "I'm just asking you something important."

"If it's like that all the time, we may never leave this bed. I mean, I am seriously worn out. And sore. But I'll deny that I said that if you were to tell someone." She promised him that his secrets were safe with her. "Thank you. But honestly, that's the best sex I've ever had. In all my life."

"That's all you need to say about that." She put her fingers over his mouth, and he took the opportunity to kiss them. "I think maybe we might have to wait until the kids move out before we have that loud of sex again. My bear is just lying in the corner of her space, exhausted but smiling. She's forever smiling."

"Thank you. My bear is strutting around like he's won the world cup of all sex." He tickled her when she told him it wasn't that good. "You know that I'm right. That was the best."

"Yes, it was. Now shut up so that I can take a quick nap. It's almost five in the morning, and the kids will be back around ten." He told her that he'd spoken to his brother yesterday, and he knew not to bring them back unless he called them. "So they'll all know that we've had sex. Right?"

"Yes. Especially Mark. He's more than likely

marking in his book how many times you came and how many times you made me come, too. It's a — hey, that wasn't nice. Give me back the covers, or I'll have to put my cold feet on you. I will, so don't tempt me."

For the rest of the morning, they talked about different things. He told her about being immortal, and she told him that she had some money that they could share, too. After telling her his worth, she told him she was keeping her money to buy things that he'd never know about.

"That's a good idea. I go over the accounts when I get a bill from them so that no one is tricking me into any services that I don't need. Amelia taught us that when she became a part of the family. Or it could have been Jamie. I don't remember. But it has kept us on the straight and narrow about keeping our records straight. I have enough on my mind without worrying about someone double charging me for something that I've purchased." Trinity told him that she did her own taxes as well. "Oh, not me. We have some accountants that do ours. It's too many charities and income from rentals that I would definitely screw up if left in charge of that. Then there is us as a family that we have to take care of as well. Yeah, too much for one person to think they'd have a handle on, I think."

They spoke about a few other things as they drifted in and out of sleep. By the time the sun was fully in the sky, they were both in the kitchen having a light breakfast of croissants and jelly. He had a cup of hot tea with his and Trinity was having a tall glass of juice. He told her that she'd have to drink a great deal more now that they had bonded, as the magic that they had would wear them out sooner if they didn't.

Once they ate what they wanted, she headed to her office to take care of the things that she had to work on, and he did the same. The winery was doing well and he'd gotten his shipment of corks in just yesterday. He was thrilled to be able to have a smooth transition from white wine to the red that sold much better than anything else.

"You busy?" He looked up, lost for a few seconds in his thoughts, when his brother, Frazier, showed up outside the storage barn he owned, too. "I have several questions, but I have information as well. First of all, the paperwork came through on Patty. She's officially yours. We heard from the judge last night and he said that he'd just go ahead and file it. None of the kids were shown to have any relatives out there that the judge thought the kids would be better off with."

"That's great news. When we get them back tonight, we'll have a celebration about it. The other kids wanted to wait to have a party until all of them were adopted." He shook his head. "I'm the father of six of the most wonderful females and the best little boy. I'm so fucking lucky."

"You are." He asked him what else he had for him. "Nothing earth-shattering. But the man who was trying his level best to buy you out a few months ago is in jail. His boss made sure that he knew what it was all about, too. They would like to talk to you about expanding but I told him that now wasn't the best time as you'd only just gotten married. I hope that was all right."

"It is, thank you. I really needed this time with Trinity. Not just for the sex, though that was mind-blowing, but we talked about a great many things too. The kids were the most important conversation. However, we decided that we have enough kids. I don't know that later we'll change our mind but that's where we are now." He asked him what else he had. "I mean, I'm feeling pretty good now, so lay whatever you're putting off on me."

"Ben has pleaded not guilty by reason of insanity. No one is buying it, especially the judge. He said that he wants the victims of his shit put out there for everyone to know about. I think that once he's in prison, he won't last all that long. The judge has received several messages from inmates wanting Ben to be their cell mate. I doubt very much that it'll be a long stay together either." Ewing said that he didn't think that he'd go easy either. "No, I believe that you're right. He's in for a rude awakening when he gets there. His sister is suing him for wrongful death too of her son."

They talked about a few more things as he walked the line in his building. He did get around to asking his questions, nothing earth shattering as he said, but just general information and then asked him if he'd donate to the basket that Grannie's store was auctioning off.

"It's for the scholarship money that we set up at the store for kids to apply for. I didn't get a good number, but Maddy was saying that there were over four thousand applicants as it was now.

I don't know what to say to that. Other than I need to ask you guys if you want to award two of them rather than the one for the first year." Ewing told his brother he was all for that, and if they didn't have enough money, he'd be willing to donate more. "Thanks. Anyway, the basket idea came from one of your kids as a matter of fact. Patty said that they had raffles at the grocery store they used to steal from. Did you know that she kept an accounting of how much they stole? She's a good kid and I have a feeling she's going to go far in life."

Ewing had to agree. He had been helping her with her homework for the past several nights to get her caught up and he thought that she was smarter than the little girl thought she was too. She hadn't had a great deal of positive reinforcement in her life, and he was going to make sure that she knew just how proud he was of her.

After his brother left him, Ewing decided that he'd gotten as much done as he could. The popping in and out thing was much more useful than he'd ever imagined it would be. He could be at home, pop to one of his many businesses, and be home in time for dinner.

He also loved that he was dressed after shifting. This morning he'd tested that theory when one of the faeries had asked him several times if he was all right. Shifting to his bear and back again, he didn't have as many kinks to work out as he did before.

Also, with the shifting, he realized too that his bear was a bit bigger. Not so noticeable as a human but when he'd been his bear, it was obvious to him that he was at least several inches taller as well as his bear seemed to be wider across the chest than he'd been before sex. That's what he was basing everything on before sex and after sex. He was laughing as he made his way into the house after getting there.

"You have to find a way to make this work, please." He didn't enter the office but listened to Patty talk to someone. It only took him several seconds before he realized that she was speaking to her mom. "The teacher won't let me call the others sisters and brothers because our last name is different. And she said that until the court man tells us to, I'm not allowed to call you Mom either. That's not fair."

"What's her name?" He could hear the anger

in Trinity's voice when she asked Patty who that was. After getting the name, she told her that she'd take care of it. That was when Ewing decided to make himself known. "There's your dad now. You tell him what this teacher said to you, and we'll see what his opinion is about this mess."

"You're our daughter. I wanted to put that out there first. Judge Hartman called my brother this morning and told him. And the paperwork has been filed as well. You are officially our daughter as are the rest of the family." Patty hugged him, sobbing about how much better her life was going to be now. "It might not be right away if your mother goes down to the school and tells them off."

"She won't do that." Patty turned and looked at Trinity. "You won't do that, will you? Cause trouble at the school? I don't care if you do or not, but I'm betting that you have a lot to say to Mrs. Spiegel."

"I can make that promise. But when she hurts any of my children, whether we have the paperwork or not, she's messing with me." Patty looked at him and he could see just the beginnings of a twinkle in her eyes. "I won't do this if you don't agree that I should. But think about this. She might be doing this to other children, too, and I can't stand for some other adopted kid—like you six, including little Billy see them suffer needlessly about some woman that needs to have her head straightened out by me."

Patty looked at him and then back at her mom. Ewing knew that she was having a hard time deciding it or not, whether to allow her mom to kick some ass or just to let it go. He knew better than to put his opinion in but waited for her to decide.

"It would be better if she was made to know that the things that she's been saying is wrong, won't it?" Trinity told her that it would make a lot of difference to a lot of people. "All right. But don't kill her. I think that I'd not want to see you in prison. You'd hurt other people. Just be nice if you can."

"I will be if I can." When Patty left them, Trinity was picking up her phone. "I'm going to get this over with if it's the last thing I do today. No one is going to pick on my children."

Ewing didn't stick around. He knew that as soon as she was fired up, he'd start laughing, and that would get him into trouble as well. Making his way to the baby's room, he picked up little Billy and kissed his face. It surprised him when he kept trying to turn his head to the right, looking in the corner.

"Can you see someone there, little buddy?" He turned him around so that he could look in the corner better. "Who do you see? Someone coming to visit you?"

He didn't have any idea why, but he thought perhaps that he was seeing a ghost. When he'd spoken to the other women about how sometimes it looked like Billy was staring at someone and cooed a great deal. Even for him being just an infant, he was sure that was it. He didn't want to freak anyone else out, so he kept that part to himself.

"You tell whomever that is that you're going to be a good boy for them and talk to them whenever they come around." Billy turned to him, looking into his eyes. It was then that he thought that Billy could understand him. And he also knew that whomever it was he was having a conversation with was going to be some lost family member that he'd missed. Perhaps his mom or dad had come to see him.

He wanted to think that after all this time his parents were still around. And the thought of them looking over his children made him feel particularly good about life in general. He also hoped that Grannie and Grandda were about as well. It would have tickled them both to no end to see such a little fighter living on their mountain top.

He'd heard all his life that babies could see and hear things that adults didn't. It wouldn't surprise him in the least bit that Billy could do all kinds of things. They had only just realized that by helping him stay alive, they had inadvertently changed him into a bear. It was fine by the family, but he did worry that if anyone had come for him, they'd be pissed off about it. But now he didn't have to worry about it at all. Billy was their son, and they were going to show him how to be the best bear cub there was.

"You tell them, or it whatever they are, that you're well loved and taken care of. There is no point in haunting us because we have you and your sisters taken well care of." Kissing the little man on the forehead, he looked into the corner, too.

"Whoever you are, if you're here, I love this little boy with all that I am, and I won't have you scaring him or making him do things that he shouldn't be doing. He's my son, and I will protect him with my life, even if I have to go to the ends of the earth to find you and make you pay for upsetting him."

Chapter 7

By the end of the year, things were going as well as they expected them to. The kids, all of them, were growing up so fast, and Billy was crawling now. As soon as someone put him on the floor, the little boy was off getting his toys from the toy box or hanging out with one of his sisters. Even they were doing well with having him around under foot nowadays.

Ewing didn't worry about the family. Theirs nor his brothers' families. They were all doing well and he thought that with all that was going on, he felt as if Trinity had been born to the mountain and that she'd been in his life forever. It was a wonderful feeling, having hearth and home, and he couldn't have been more thrilled when the tree was up in their living room, and the kids were experiencing their first Christmas with them.

Thanksgiving had been a wonderful holiday. They'd celebrated at Mark's home, and the faeries had made it their job to make sure that everyone had what they wanted to eat and drink. The turkey, a fresh bird, had made a huge hit, and the girls — or perhaps they didn't know — didn't seem to mind that they were eating Rocky the Turkey. Ewing wasn't going to spoil their fun with the meal, but he was sure that they'd be asking questions after he seemingly disappeared from the pen.

There were still men surrounding the area that had been used for the killing spree. As it turned out, twenty-six men and women had been arrested in the sting to get those who had actually done the killing taken care of. Without the help of Amelia, they might never have had any luck in bringing them to justice. It did bother the townspeople to know that their own mayor had been a part of the group that enjoyed — sickly — killing off teenage girls when he had four of his own.

"I just heard from the prison. Ben is dead. They said that it looks as if he took his own life, but I feel that they have that wrong. I'm betting that they didn't look all that hard in finding out if he'd been murdered. Just one less thing that needed to be worried about is what I think." Trinity told Ewing that she would tell the girls later as they were at the pack house today making gifts for the family. "I have a few of the ornaments that we made when Grannie would send us there for a few days. I thought it was because she wanted some quiet time but the more I miss my kids for being there, the more I realize that she was helping us get to know other groups of shifters better. Did I tell you that I love you today? I do."

"And I love you so much." She pulled the next batch of cookies out of the oven. Before they were even on the cooling rack that she had out, the faeries were decorating them. They were beautifully done. He'd say that for them. "The kids and I baked our cookies yesterday and decorated them. This batch is just for the faeries. I've never seen even a child have as much fun as they seem to be having. And they look picture perfect, too."

"I did see that you showed them what cookies looked like. Do they know that they can branch out, too? Make their own designs." She only had to hand him one of the cookies that he guessed the faeries had decorated on their own. It was so thick with icing and sprinkles that he doubted that it would taste all that good. And he'd bet anything that it weighed about a pound, too. Putting it back in the cookie jar with the others, he sat down and watched the cookies being made. "So, can I have one?"

"Sure, but just so you know, you're going to have to try everyone of them that is in here decorating. To make sure that you get the best cookie they've made." Sometimes, like a great deal of late, he thought that having such competitive creatures around would get him into trouble. Of course, that's what he had Trinity for. To keep him from weighing a ton by now as well. "I do have some water in the kettle if you'd like some tea. I could use a nice cup of it but without sugar. Things are just too sweet around here for me to think that I need anything else."

After enjoying a cup of tea each, he did get to have a cookie without the frosting. It had broken when Trinity had dropped it onto the cooling racks and he said he'd eat it. He was really glad that he was losing the war with himself not to grab one and have one.

While cleaning up the kitchen after the cookies were all decorated, he helped box up the newly made cookies into containers to give away. The Grand Witch, namely Amelia, was going to get a lot of them because of who she was to the little people, but they'd also have more than enough to give to the families that came around singing carols over the next few nights.

Each faerie was able to take one of their creations home with them to have the sugar fix. He didn't know if they got the zoomies like the kids did when they got too much sugar or not. And didn't want to be around them if they did.

Dinner was just going to be the two of them, and they decided that it would be just as easy for them to grill out a couple of steaks. There were potatoes put in the already hot oven, and the bread that had been made just this morning was going to accompany their meal. Cookies would be for dessert.

They had a television in the living room. It was a huge one that took up most of the upper wall space over the fireplace. After making a fire for the two of them, they sat in the relatively dark room but for the lights on the Christmas tree. The faeries had helped decorate it as well, and he was glad to see that the lights, colorful ones, were the perfect light for their big room.

"I heard from my parents. They're coming, but my brothers aren't. To be honest with you, I'm glad that they're not. They can smoke pot at home and have no trouble trying to have some when they're out, too. Mom said that they couldn't wait to spend some time with the kids and that they had gone overboard with gifts for them all. I told her that we'd done the same thing, it was their first Christmas together, and they all went all out in all the Cross homes."

"Did you talk to them about moving here?" She told Ewing that she'd not had to. Her mom had mentioned that now that they had grandchildren, it was time they got out of that big house and got something smaller and closer to them. "Good. I'm also glad that they don't have any problem with treating them all the same, either. Just like us, they think of them as nothing but blood children. I'm happy about the fact that we don't have to browbeat them into spending time with them. I don't know who has more fun, them or the kids."

"I will say this. They were never like this when I was a kid. It was more survival of the fittest around them. Now they're getting down on the floor and having a good time with them. I never thought that they'd have this much fun. And my dad, he loves them to pieces." He noticed, too, that Billy was a big hit with the older couple as well. "I almost forgot to tell you. The shop, A Cross to Bear, will be closed after the new year to have the flooring replaced. I hadn't realized how worn it was until I nearly lost my footing when I tripped on a carpet snag. The men said that it should only take a couple of weeks, and by then the painters will be able to get their job finished as well. Also, the new roof. Are you sure your brothers are all right with spending that much money on the building?"

"That was Grannie's pride and joy. I'm betting that any one of them would spend twice that much on it just to have it looking good. Also, you said that you were going to hire more help to have more than one checkout lane. I love that idea and when I brought it up to the others, they said they liked it as well." They talked about this and that, and Ewing could feel himself falling asleep.

The room was warm and cozy. The fire was soothing to his senses. When he felt himself completely drift all, he welcomed it with open arms. Christ, he'd been exhausted all week and was glad for some downtime while the children were away.

Billy was cooing in the middle of the floor when he opened his eyes. He wasn't sure what woke him up but he was glad that he could enjoy the little boy talking and cooing to someone in the corner of the room. He'd been delighted and surprised that none of the children bothered the tree. No ornaments had been spilled off it, nor had there been any paper wrestling when they were trying to be sneaky.

"Hey, big boy. What's going on?" He looked at him and smiled. It was all he needed to be able to power through the day when he thought about what a simple smile could do for him. "Are you talking to someone?"

He looked around the living room and especially hard at the places that Billy seemed to be staring at the most. When he came to him, crawling on his hands and knees, he picked him up and put him on his chest. He laid his head on him and closed his eyes. Ewing decided to join him in a little longer nap.

When he woke up the second time, not only

was Billy still on his chest but he was still sleeping as well. He'd gotten to the point that he was taking baby food now, and the doctors couldn't believe how well he was doing after having such a scare when he'd been tiny. And he had been a tiny little man, too.

Rolling to the floor, leaving Billy on the couch, he took one of the cushions off the other end and put it on the floor, too. Just in the event that he rolled himself over and off the couch. He was getting really good at surprising them about his development.

"I hope that it's you, Grannie, that is watching over Billy. I miss you so much but just to think about him being able to meet you makes me hurt a little less that you're not here any longer." He watched the corner that Billy had been staring at the most. "If it's you Mom and Dad, I'm glad that you're here too. I don't remember you all that much, couldn't even pick out your picture if not for the ones on the walls here but I'm happy to know, or think I know that you're here for my children."

He sat there for the longest time. Not really thinking about any one thing but thinking about his family. Ewing had been told his entire life that things were the way that they were because they had to be. But glad that his parents were gone hurt him to think about. He just wished he'd had longer with them than he had.

Ewing had been the youngest of all the brothers. He'd been about six months old when his father had died with his mom. Grannie had never thought that they'd done them right, leaving them in a house without food or water to care for them. Oftentimes, he thought perhaps that they had hoped that they'd died too to be with them in a sick sort of way. He'd never told his brothers that nor his grannie but that was how he felt about them.

If not for Grandda, they might have gone on thinking that the two of them, his parents, had died together. But it wasn't so. When his mom found out that their father was gone, she thought that she could leave the mountain. But being saddled with six children, all of them younger than his own kids were at the time, didn't appeal to her. Or something like that, he thought. He had never wanted to think of her as being selfish but having his own family now, that's all he could think about. Is how selfish she'd been in not being a part of their lives.

His father had had an accident that resulted in his death, and his mother had taken her own life. He could never do that to his own children, even for as much as he loved his Trinity.

In order to keep the land that they had lived on for all their lives, a Cross had to be living there even if they were the last man standing, so to speak. If not, then it would revert to the park, and more than likely, everything that they had would have been left where they left it, including farm equipment and the like.

He couldn't see anyone leaving the land willingly. They all had enough money of their own, and they invested too in the towns surrounding them. And when it was necessary they would pitch in whatever help was needed when the town needed them too. It was a win-win as far as he was concerned.

They could come and go as they pleased; they didn't have to occupy the mountain twenty-four-seven. Just live here. He knew that he would. Simply because it was the best place that he knew of and an even more wonderful place to raise kids. They had freedoms that city children would never have. The freedom of all the outdoors.

~*~

Trinity loved working outside. Even though it was snowing and fairly cold, she still loved being out where she could have the sunshine on her face and the warmth of it as well. As she was making her way to the barn, having only just been able to get a milking cow, she let the chickens out and told them to be careful. Yes, she thought to herself, she was talking to the barn animals.

"Mom?" She smiled at Patty. "I was wondering if you think I'm old enough to learn how to milk Caroline."

"I don't see why not. I mean, she's a good old girl, and her temperament is fine. We'll give it a try. If your hands aren't big enough, we'll try again later." She sat her daughter—oh, how she loved the sound of that coming from her mouth—on the stool that she usually used and showed her how to get Caroline ready.

"If your hands are too cold, she's going to object to you touching her. Just be careful." After getting her hands washed up and disinfected, they did the same to the udders. "Now, I've shown you before how you have to milk her from the top to the bottom. Once you get the hang of it, you'll wonder what all the fuss was about. Go ahead and get started."

The first spray of milk coming from the cow had Patty squealing with delight. But it upset Caroline a bit, so Trinity showed her how to talk nicely to her, and she'd be fine. It was a rare treat for her to see Patty so determined to do something around the farm. Of late, she'd been blowing off her chores in favor of reading books. It was hard to tell her to put them down and do her work, but they were working around that, too.

Caroline was milked, although a little later than normal, and they took the fresh milk into the house. After it was set up and put away by the faeries, the two of them, with the other girls went out to gather eggs. They didn't get many this time of year, but they still gathered what was in the nesting bins. They were all shocked when they found a tiny chick, about four or five hours old, huddling up to her momma in the warm barn. They decided to call her Snowball.

All the animals that they used on the farm had names, thanks mostly to do with her daughters. And each animal was addressed by their names daily and the girls would act like they'd missed them through the night too. It was silly, she knew, but it also brightened up her day to know that the kids cared so much for the animals that they were in charge of.

Not only did they have cows and chickens but they had pigs and goats too. The animals that were around rarely bothered the animals that were in pens, so she was glad for that. If one of the animals came up missing, it was because whatever had taken it must have been starving, as the mountain animals had a deep respect for the Cross family and wouldn't do that unless there was a reason.

Once all the outdoor chores were finished up, they'd gotten about a dozen eggs this morning, she started on breakfast for the girls. It was something that she enjoyed more than anything she did with them as they talked to her and each other, and that was how she found out the most interesting things.

Ewing came in the back door when she was ready to put the plates together. He'd gone out with his brothers to find a missing child. It happened all the time around the mountains for one reason or another, and all she could think about was the little boy whose parents had tossed him over the side of one of the many falls to kill him off. Their plan was to sue the park for negligence, but the Rangers, all of them had been park rangers for a long time, and he was safely taken from his parents as well as the other children in the home.

Trinity only had to look at Ewing to know that it hadn't gone well. She sent him up to get Billy so that he could have some eggs with them as well. It would do Ewing a world of good to be around the little boy as he wouldn't comment on things but would just jabber away about whatever baby talk he was using.

"Billy said that he wants to go into town and see the Christmas lights tonight. Who wants to go with him?" Of course, the girls wanted to do that. She was surprised that he even had to ask.

They'd taken the trip to see lights several times so far in the season. The first time they went, there weren't as many lights up as there were decorations around the storefronts. But each time they went, they saw more and more lights, and it was so much fun to see the animatronics working, too. There were a great many of them depicting bears climbing one thing or another.

After getting them off to school and Billy

down for his early morning nap, she went to her office to take care of the paperwork that the president had sent her to go over. He would send her his speeches early enough that she could go over them, clearing up anything that didn't flow well and any kind of comments that he made that he shouldn't have.

Finishing up after a few hours, she went to the kitchen for a much-needed cup of tea and something to tide her over until lunch. Mae came to tell her what was going on in the household, little things like they'd need shampoo for one of the girls. There was a leaky window in one of the bedrooms.

Usually, they took care of those things themselves, the faeries having so much magic, but today, she'd run into a problem that she'd never encountered before. Following the little person up the stairs, she entered the big room that had been set aside for just the faeries and knew immediately that it was something that she was going to need help with. One of the large windows had broken when a large limb from the tree next to the house broke off and crashed into the room.

"We can make the large limb disappear, but

it would be someplace we'd not need it to be. The glass is easy enough to fix, but the faeries aren't sure what sort of glass you'd like to have in it. They seem to think that making it colorful will be fine with you." She said that it normally would, but she'd have to check with Ewing. "He is back now from taking the children to school. Oh, how I wish I could go with them. Don't you think it would be fun to be able to learn all day long?

She doubted very much any learning would be done if a bunch of faeries showed up to class and were flitting about the room. No, she thought, it would not be fun to go to school all day with the faeries.

When Ewing looked over the mess that had been made, he was upset about all the breakage. Not that they could have foreseen something like this happening, but two of the little people had been hurt, and he felt responsible for it. Getting the limb out, they were surprised then by how much damage had been done to the house, too.

"I'm going to tell you how we're going to get this done. Nothing nor anyone is to deviate from the plan, all right?" Ewing was trying his best not to laugh. The faeries were nearly vibrating the house off its foundation by the way that they were energized to work with him. After doing the steps, removing the glass one piece at a time, he then went out of doors to survey the damage there. After giving the little creatures a list of things that they'd have to do and in order of them being done, he allowed them to make the windows in this room all colorful if they wished. So long as everyone had a chance to do something to some part of the windows.

The two of them left before the windows were finished being decorated. They were nearly down the stairs when he felt Amelia show up in the room. She'd just bet that she was having a fit over something, or she was making sure that the two little faeries were all right. For as much as she was a hard ass, Amelia was about as soft as she could be when it came to all her domain.

The rest of the morning and into the afternoon, she was busy with the household. A house this big needed a large staff and while she was glad to have them, she thought that sometimes they made more work than they needed to. Cleaning the fireplaces had become a daily thing for the staff, and while she didn't care when they were cleaned, they usually ended up having a dust fight, and the entire room would be sooty. She wasn't sure, but Trinity thought that they did that because they enjoyed cleaning up after themselves. It could have been worse, she thought to herself, but they were happy, and so was she.

Dinner tonight was going to be quick. It was nearly getting dark by the time the girls made it home from school nowadays. But soon, the time would be for all daylight they could manage and more outdoor fun for them all. Trinity was looking forward to going tea blossom hunting with the girls and the other children of the bruin. By the time there was full darkness outside, they were loaded up in the jeep and out looking at the beautiful lights that were nearly on every lamp post and business front. There were houses, too, but they wouldn't be able to shine bright without the town. It was just spectacular the way they all seemed to get together to make their town beautiful.

They'd given out two scholarships this past fall. The students that had received them were overjoyed by them. So were their parents. Twenty thousand dollars was given away and the kids that received them wouldn't have to work while going to college. She thought that it was great in that part alone.

She was just stepping out of the shower, her second one of the day, when Ewing joined her in the room. Wrapping the large towel around her breasts and body, she asked him if everything was all right.

"Not now that you've covered up, it's not." The two of them had been teasing each other for the last few days. It was difficult to have sex during the day as there was someone always underfoot. Today, with Billy with the faeries and his nanny, they had just very little time to spare before the girls had to be picked up from school. Dropping the towel on the floor, she raced him to the bed, and that was where they ended up together, just as his phone was going off.

"Don't answer it." He said that he wasn't going to, but she could tell that he did indeed need to answer the phone. Riding her body up against his, he moaned loudly and told her to behave. She wasn't going to let this opportunity go without a fight.

Tearing his buttons off, she took one of his hard nipples into her mouth and suckled at it hard.

Then, when she nipped at him, biting gently on his nipple, she could hear his frustration as he spoke on the phone. Getting up from the bed, not being bashful at all about her nudity, she sat down in front of him and undid his belt, and then the snap at the top of his jeans.

Trinity made short work of his boxers. Pulling them down over the crown of his cock, she slid her tongue over the top of his cock and was rewarded with the tiniest drop of cum. Licking him more, pulling his pants off when he finally lifted his hips. She swallowed his cock down past the tightness of her throat as she fondled his balls.

She knew that she was playing dirty and didn't care. He was going to remember this the next time he came for her and his phone rang. The phone was tossed across the room. Once it hit the wall, her body seemed to come apart with just the sound of his frustrations and the breaking glass of the thing.

"I'm going to beat your ass for that. I needed to take that call." He might well have needed it but she could tell that he didn't much care if he did or not. He slapped his hand onto her ass, and she came a second time, her body hurting with the pain and pleasure like nothing had before. "You like that, do you? Well, I'm going to have me some—holy Christ Trinity, yes."

All she'd done was to give his tender balls a small jerk. They were warm and full, and she wanted to tease him a bit. But when he started coming, holding her head down over his cock while he fucked her mouth, Trinity wasn't prepared for the amount of cum that she had to swallow and was disappointed that she'd missed a bit of him. It was the best way possible to have sex with someone, she thought and squealed when she was suddenly airborne, bouncing a couple of times before lying on the bed beneath him.

He took her hard, his cock filling her, slapping his balls onto her pussy with each downward stroke. It was hard and dirty, and she wouldn't have it any other way right now. Each time he took her, she raised up her ass so that he could take her deeper, harder than before. Even while she was holding onto his arms, clinging to him so that she'd not shatter apart, her body was racing to meet up with his. His need to dominate her was more than she could take, and she screamed when he bit down on her throat.

Nothing could have prepared her for the way it turned her body inside out and then seemingly upside down. She felt herself being pulled through a small hole and then back through the other side as he suckled at the wound he created at her throat. There was no pain after a few minutes, only pleasure. More pleasure than she'd had in some time with Ewing, and it nearly was too much.

Whatever he was doing, whatever he was feeling by making love to her this way, she would take it ten times more than she thought that she could, if only to satisfy him. Trinity loved Ewing with all that she was and knew that he did the same for her.

Christ, he was laying claim to her like he'd never done to her before. And before she could realize that she was coming again, her body seemed to have been slapped upside of it, and she was out for the count.

When she woke, she was snuggled around Ewing and he was speaking softly. She didn't understand that he was talking to her until he asked her if she was all right and that he was sorry that he'd hurt her so badly. Lifting her face up to look at him, she could see the tears on his face and wondered aloud about them.

"I thought that I'd nearly killed you." She said that she was fucking fantastic. "Yes, but when you passed out for so long, I was worried about you. Are you really all right?"

"I am. I'm with you and that right there is enough for me to be able to enjoy you for the rest of my days." He kissed her gently on her lips, and she smiled at him. "I'm sorry about your call. Not really, but I thought that I'd just say that to you."

"I don't even remember who it was now." She snuggled under his chin and thought that she could sleep like this forever. Then her alarm went off and she knew she was going to have to get up and go get the kids. "Duty calls."

"You take a nap, and I'll go get them. I have a few things at the post office that I need to pick up anyway. That way, we don't have to make two trips. The weather is supposed to be worse by this evening, and I'm looking forward to the weekend here with you and the family." She didn't argue with him but rolled over, taking most of the blankets with her when he got up. "I guess that's a yes. You'll see me later."

"It is. Don't forget to check on the lunch

situation while there. Also...you know what? I should go with you. I have a list of things that I have to ask the teachers about their homework. Never a dull moment around here, is it?"

After getting the kids, they stopped and got pizza. There were a lot of people without power, so they invited anyone who needed it to use their generators. They might well should have been without power, too, but the faeries would make sure they weren't without anything.

Stopping at the post office and getting about a half a dozen boxes, they were headed home. Trinity listened to the kids talking about their Christmas break and all the things they were going to do. She let the sounds of family roll around her, and when they got home, she hugged all of the kids tightly. Trinity felt like she was the luckiest person and mom in the world.

Chapter 8

Ten years later.

Billy sat very still, listening to the others speaking in the room. He could see them, could even have a conversation with them, but he, like any smart man would do, knew that at a moment's notice or none at all really that bears could and would get angry about how things were put to paper while he was with them. They wanted things to be right and that meant that names were spelled correctly and the order in which you're telling it was exact as well. One of the elders looked at him.

"You getting this down, young man? You should be making sure that this is all right rather than sitting there like a bump on a log." Billy told the most senior bear there today that he was and wrote down the names of the three other bears that were with him. They were brothers born of the same parents that had been living here just as bears before the queen of earth had given them magic. "Ezekiel said that you have a contraption that will record us. If'n you do, I don't want to talk into it. Might steal my voice or something. I won't be able to roar to keep me safe if that happens. No, you don't go recording me, all right? And there won't be none of those picture things like you've got either. I have my soul, and that's all. You mind your p's and q's, you hear me?"

He'd had to test the theory if he could or couldn't record their voices. He could, but he had to hide the recorder because they'd spend too much time on speculating on how it worked rather than talking to him about the mountain and the families that had been long since gone. By the time he got them to settle down and have a conversation with them, they'd be too worn out to do what he'd summoned them for. Billy could do that, too. Summon anyone that he wished to speak to that hadn't as yet moved on. It seemed like all the bears from the beginning stuck around. They loved watching their families figure out the mountain and what treasures it could give them.

These bears, the first of many that had come to the land now known as the Great Smoky Mountains, had the territory all laid out so that they and their families wouldn't be hunted by the tribes that shared the land with them.

"You need some pictures too?" He asked Ezekiel if they knew where he could find them, knowing that if they would tell him when it was mentioned that he could go and find them rather than wait a week or two for them to remember where they'd hidden their treasures. He'd found a lot of their 'treasures' while talking to the first family than he ever thought possible. "They're in that big cave where I showed you before. You know the one? It's got a lot of junk in there too but the pictures were boxed up real nice."

The cave, one of the largest ones he'd ever been in so far, hadn't been investigated by the park's people so far. Not for thousands of years had anyone other than himself and his family been in the cave that had stored so much information as that one did.

Writings on the walls were made with ash from a burnt stick. There were drawings, too, most of which he'd had to have explained to him.

They'd been made and colored even with smashed leaves and berries.

He'd also been able to unearth a great many geo and hard stones that turned out to be diamonds and emeralds. Not to say that there wasn't junk in there, too. A tree branch that had fallen on one of the little bears and killed him had been saved. There were bits and pieces of the forest that they had decided were pretty or maybe someday useful. Other things like that, as well. What depressed him the most was that they thought if they were to put things in the large cave, nothing would bother them. They'd been so wrong. Books and pictures had been put on the wayside.

Things like moles and even smaller creatures had gotten in and made a mess of things. The one thing that he had thought the saddest was the wedding dress that had belonged to a long lost relative that only wanted to keep it nice for their own daughters.

They did find caves that had been homes of some of the tribespeople, humans just passing through, and even the few hundred people who had decided, for one reason or another, to live out their lives in the caves. He'd known of two such people, meeting them when he'd been out looking for information. Even as new as a month ago had he known someone who was hiding from one form of law or the other as well.

"I found the cave that you're talking about. My dad and uncles are helping me clear it out before the park comes across it. The park will keep everything that they find, and I don't want that to happen, at least not until I finish with them. The park will put them on display for everyone to see, but for this, our family. The things in there are family and that's the only place that they should be. In the family." Jameson, another of the original shifter bears had asked him if there had been any people living in the cave that they'd been using. "No, no humans. But I did find the bodies of your parents like you said that I would."

Nodding, no one asked him if they'd moved them. They wouldn't. Where they had lived and died was where they decided they'd stay. He likened that to having their own little cemetery in the cave. Jameson then asked him what he knew about the queen of the earth.

"Nothing more than you've told me. I've met her, of course, you know that. And you all have to give me permission to ask her what she'd done that day and why. That's the only reason that I'm asking you. So I have a good record of the day that she gave you all the magic to walk and talk with man." Benjamin, the very first bear shifter, said that he'd give him permission, being the oldest, that would make it so. "I won't go to her with only one of you giving me permission, Uncle Benjamin. It's all four of you or nothing. I won't invade any information that you might not care for me having. This is a big undertaking and I don't want anyone to feel like they've been pressured into something when they didn't want it to happen. I don't want to ever have any of you coming back on me telling me that I did you wrong." His uncle just nodded.

In the end, they'd all, all the generations, had given him permission to speak to the earth queen, who had asked them to be men and bears. She wanted them to be able to live out their lives on the mountain and to show other bears, the rest of them, how to live there without being harmed. It had made it so that before, the creatures that lived there were protected by the park and had a fighting chance of surviving when man decided that they were much more useful dead than alive.

It took Billy months to gather up the information that he needed. A year of him going through dusty boxes and crates. Trunks of old pottery and finds had been the pain of his existence. He had more cobwebs in his hair, his mother told him, than most people did in the world over a weekend. But he had a desire to be able to find family information and to make it so that anyone who wanted it was able to get it, too. Then he'd been granted permission to not only speak to the earth queen but to go to her realm while he was doing it. His aunt Amelia had gained him that audience, and he would forever be grateful for her doing so much for his cause.

"I so loved the bears and what they stood for when I first saw them. To think that something so large and so scary looking could be the best of parents to their young. I loved to watch their gracefulness too in climbing mountainsides as well as trees. I also was sad that so many of them were being killed off for only their coat and how it would keep humans warm. Leaving the meat behind because they thought it too much effort to at least attempt to make sure that their families were fed as well." Lilliane, the first queen of earth, had not just made it so that bears could walk among the humans but wolves and cats as well. "We have all learned a great deal from their counterparts. Man and beast can live together if they wish, but for a time, it wasn't unheard of for humans to kill off their neighbor simply because they were a beast, too. Such a tragic ending that my animals had to go into hiding for so long that I feared that there would never be peace between them."

"What kind of magic did you have to use? That's the question that most of them ask. Not the exact knowledge, but basically why you chose some bear families over others. And what is your strongest family now." He thought that an easy question but it wasn't for the former queen. She looked out over her own fields and stared for so long that he thought her not to answer. "You don't have to tell me, my lady. I think it was mostly for my own curiosity rather than anything else."

"It's all right, young Billy. I shall answer." She smiled at him then. "Hands down, my greatest creation would be the Cross bears. Not only did they take the magic that was given to them and make it better, but they never harmed others or other families with the knowledge that they had.

Also, they would help any of the other creatures. Be they bear or cougar, the Cross bears were one that could be depended on. All throughout the years." It made him proud to be known as a Cross bear.

Even though he'd been changed when he'd been nothing more than a small child, his pride was there. It was the only thing that had saved him, everyone thought when they heard the story of his coming to the family.

It took him several months to get all the information in order. Pictures, too, were put aside that he wanted for the book. No one would read it, he thought, but for the family. He was fine with that, too. So long as the words were put out there where anyone and everyone with the last name Cross could see where their family had come from and how they'd prospered over the decades.

The pictures were his friend. Since he could go back and talk to the people in them, he had a firsthand accounting of the day. Sometimes, they'd put someone up for the night as they were thinking to get pictures of the falls they'd only heard about. The price of a picture would be a great deal to those that had wanted one so to be able to trade for it made it seem all the more special.

Once word got out about the hospitality of the Cross Mountain people, others showed up for a night's stay for the price of whatever wears they'd been hawking. A pretty tin can with candies in it. Yards of fabric that the man was going to sell to the tribes once he made it to them. Even though they had all the meat that they wanted, they would trade for a night's stay with a meal for some fish caught in the many lakes and rivers.

Seeds were a big thing too to trade. That was how the family still had tomatoes and corn, trading with the tribes when they were able to get them. Furs, too, of other animals around were traded for wood to light a couple of fires. Even magic was traded from one person to the next and had value like nothing else.

Billy took an entire year to write the first installment of the Cross family. He'd been thrilled, too, when he'd unearthed a cookbook written in the hand of the person who had perfected the recipe. Other tidbits as well. How to get molasses and honey. The best way to light a fire without smoking yourself out. How to mend pants and shoes. The best way to sharpen a knife. It was all in there. Every bit of the information that he found and was able to shed some light on, he put it in the book.

Alas, he'd been sad when it all wouldn't fit into the first book. His partner had been excited when he'd been upset about how much stuff was left untold. She wanted him to write many books, some of them with only information about the first bears and their families or simply a book of recipes that he'd been given on how to make a year's worth of living and eating from his finds. Bits and pieces of it had been there in the first book with just enough information.

~*~

Twenty more years later.

Billy didn't touch the box that was on his table. It had been delivered about an hour ago and sat there where he'd put it since then. He knew what was in it, the 'from' address as clear as it was to him who was to receive it. There was a box knife sitting next to it, along with a small trash bag for whatever trash might be in it. Mostly, it would be packing material, but he didn't want to make a mess when opening it after his guest arrived.

"Do you think she'll come to see you today? She didn't come the last time you had a box." He looked at his wife and mate of eleven months and told her that she would be there. That the other box hadn't had much to do with her. And that she would know today's delivery was a big deal for them both. "I hope you have a good visit with her. I know how much you miss getting to see her." She kissed him on the mouth quickly. "I'll be back this evening. I have a great deal of paperwork that needs to be done, as well as some filing on the sale sheets that we've made this week."

After telling her that he loved her, hugging both her and their child that Margo still carried, he made his way back into the kitchen to wait. He thought that the waiting was much better than it used to be before. He supposed it was because they'd been together so many times that he felt like she'd never leave him.

He knew that he'd never leave her.

The two of them had formed a bond long before he'd been living with the Cross family. He wasn't even a day old. Billy also thought that he'd had one with her long before that, even before he'd been born. But now it was different. He could speak to her now, and he loved that more than anything in the world. Besides his wife and soon-to-be child coming to him.

He looked around the room, the room that had been here for longer than most of the other nineteenth generation of Crosses. The meeting place in all the homes that were built on the mountain. That's what made this one so special. It had been meeting and greeting people for more generations than most of the people around here even thought about anymore.

And he knew them all now. Billy had talked to most of them even before the idea of a book had come to them. It became just what he wanted it to be. A history of not just the people that were living on the land now but all the generations back of Cross bears and how they had become the first shifter bears that were ever. His family.

The tightening of the room had him smiling. The power that it took to bring her to him no longer surprised nor harmed him. Turning in his seat, Billy looked at the magic that was bringing his favorite person to him, to all the people on the mountain, both gone and present.

"Why haven't you at least peeked at it?" He

looked and smiled at the little woman who had appeared before him. "I would have had that box opened up, the contents spilled all over the place, and the box out to the burn pile."

"No, you wouldn't have. You would have done the same thing if our roles were reversed. How are you, Grannie?" She told him, in her no-nonsense way, that she was dead. That was how she was. Dead as dead could be. "So you are."

When Billy was no older than a few days old, he knew somehow in his small time on this earth that he was going to die. His parents, the biological ones, whoever they were, had left him in the house that they'd brought him to because they cared more for the attention that having a child gave them than the child itself. As surly as he lay in his own wet and dirty diaper, the empty bottle at his feet, that he was not long for this world. Then, a speck flew in front of his face one day. It was then that he was able to not just put a face to the person that he'd been talking to forever but gave him hope. Something one as young as he'd been didn't have until then.

"You'll not die, young man. I won't allow it." He, unsure of his abilities to speak to her, told her that his little body was exhausted and starved. He'd been too long without anyone to love him too. "You'll not die. I have plans for the two of us. You're going to be my ears and mouth when you get to my mountain, and I won't have you leaving here without a good fight. You'll be loved up, you will. Hugged like they're hugging the stuffing out of you. I promise you, little man, you hold out, and it will be worth all the pain that you're suffering now. They'll come for you, little man. I swear it on my love for my mate. They'll come for you."

It had been three more nights and days before someone did indeed come for him, but he feared that all the promises that Grannie had made to him were for naught. He was too weak to even take a bottle now, much less be afraid of the hereafter.

With him being starved, his little body full of infection, and along with the fact that he was so dehydrated, he was ready to die. Billy—who had no name until he was brought to the hospital thought that holding on, even for the elderly woman, was too exhausting to try and live.

But live he did. And survived. His father, the man that he'd come to know as his dad, had given him some of himself so that he would live. Over the next few days, he'd see the man, Grannie had promised him that he'd be just what he needed, and he was, but over the next few days, when it looked like things were lost, his dad gave him a little more of himself every time. He could feel, even back then, that he was getting stronger and better then his mom came to give him the love that he thought that he'd miss out on. Billy was loved. Like all the other kids, he was loved.

"Now you're going to help this old woman. You don't have to. You can turn me down should you think that it's too much, and I can tell you, young Billy, that at times, I fear it will be too much, but you only have to tell me no one time, and I'll go away. Not forever. I don't have it in me to leave here when there is so much love around." She had looked in on him while his parents both of them cared for him so that he'd be where he was today.

"Billy?" He turned and looked at his grannie. Dead longer than he'd been alive but still just as spirited as he'd been told she was when she was living. Asking her if she was ready, she smiled at him. "Them others, the ghosts that you talk to. They're going to be so jealous about this today.

I've been…well, since you were a wee little one, I've been waiting for this day to come. I had me a story to tell, and you helped me tell it. Helped all of us tell it, you did. You did me proud, little Billy."

He laughed every time she said that to him since he'd grown to tower over her and outweigh her by several pounds. More than likely a hundred or so. But he loved her and what she'd give him. Peace. And her love.

"You remember the first time you told me the story of how you'd come to be born on this mountain? I had to talk to my dad then because I had knowledge that he nor my uncles had. It was then too much for my ten-year-old mind to take in but he was gentle and understanding to me." Grannie laughed. "He missed you. All of them still miss you."

"I miss them too. So very much. That day that my Alford was taken from me, I wanted to die right then and there. But there were things that I had to do, and I knew that if I left them so soon after losing the only father they ever knew, it wouldn't be good for nary a one of them. I knew that I had to make things right for them to be able to go on." He reminded her that it was doubtful that any time would have been a good time for them. "That's very true. I knew it when they were all there that while I couldn't live without my true love, they'd understand my leaving more than anyone could."

They had worked at the park. The Smoky National Park for decades. Doing the work to get paid and then later volunteering when they needed them for that. But one day, a man, a human no less, had been having a bad day and had pulled out a gun to use on all those around him. He'd not killed five little girls because Grandda had protected them with his body. Losing his own life was never anything that he ever regretted when he'd been able to save those children.

Grannie had missed him. Her sorrow, so profound, had her leaving her earthly coil behind when she decided that she'd join him. Bears, many of them bears while shifters came to the homestead, too, came to the house that night to pay homage to her and the man that she loved, letting her grandsons know that they would surely be missed.

"I think my dad took it harder than most." She nodded and while ghosts couldn't cry, she was able to do things well beyond what others had been able to do that came to see him with stories like the one that he had written. "He didn't know anyone but the two of you. His parents had died long before he could remember their faces anymore. To remember their voices. I hurt for him because I know that kind of love for a parent. I couldn't have gone on all these years without my mother's voice in my heart nor my dad's heavy hand on my shoulder."

"You're a good boy." She laughed, and he smiled. "Ewing was so afeared for you when he first heard that you could speak to the dead, especially to your grandda and I. He knew that he had to let you believe it but he wasn't willing to believe it of you just then. Then you got him to listen to you, didn't you?"

"Yes. I told him what you told me that night. That you wanted me to write a story about the mountain, and that it had to be in your words. You had me knowing things, a great many things that I wouldn't have known without you around. Such as the first family, all bears who came to claim the area as their own." She told him that he scared his daddy. "I did. And my heart hurt for that."

"But he, like the others, they came around

too. I think they enjoyed them stories more than I think people will that reads the book." She eyed the box and then looked at him. "You gonna open it, or are we just going to hope that it looks as pretty as I hope it does?"

"I'll open it for us." The box knife broke when he dropped it. He wasn't worried that it might be a bad omen. Billy had grown up with a lot of magic surrounding him and in him. His own family was more powerful alone than any one group of beings that he knew of. Once the tape was cut, he reached into the box rather than opening it up to look inside. "Oh my, Grannie."

The book, a hardback, had a cover on it. The cover picture, a picture of the homestead that he'd found, a tintype picture that had been taken when Grannie, one of the many children sitting on the front grass was only three years old. Grandda was in the picture, too, but he was a bit older, standing next to the mister of the house because he'd been there when the picture man had shown up. It had been a grand celebration, she'd told him, with them killing a hog and cooking it right up for the mountain people to enjoy.

They shared many a meal in the very spot

where the hog had been cooked. The fire just big enough to cook the meat rather than burn it had been there for weeks after that meal was done. Even the people in the small town—back then, it had consisted of a trading store, a wheelhouse for making flour, and cracked corn for the chickens. As well as an inn for people traveling through the mountain.

What amazed him and humbled him as well was that he'd spoken to all the forty-one people in the picture and could now point out any of them and tell you what their names were. How they'd died—most of them met a tragic end at a very young age—as well as when they'd been born. They had become his extended family even though none of them were related to him in any way, he still thought of them as family.

"Boy that looks like the day that it was taken. Where did I put that thing?" He told her that it had been in the big bible that she'd told him about. "That's right. It took us a long time to find it, too. I'm surely glad that I kept all that nonsense. It doesn't seem like that now, but back then, it was hard to think that anyone would care after all the time that passed. You made that list for the book, didn't you, little Billy?"

"I did. Let me have a look at it now." Going to the pictures that had been added in the middle of the thick book, he was glad that he'd insisted that the family tree be put in the storybook as well. It was huge. Families back in the day had as many children as they could afford. But one thing about living where they did, was they had plenty of meat, vegetables as well as fruits. He laid it out on the table for her to look at. "I didn't think they'd do what I wanted."

"Well, you sure did put up enough fuss about it. But I think that it was worth it. It looks just like I thought it would. Pretty, ain't it?" He had to agree. It was nice. Seeing all the names there made him feel proud of his work. But there was no way that he could have done it without all the family helping him with it. Those living and dead. "You read it to me if you've got the time. I want to hear the story out of your own voice. I need to hear it, I think.

"All right." Picking up the book, knowing that since he'd gotten a copy for everyone that lived on the mountain, he'd save this one special for his parents. After all they'd done for him, he'd be happy to let them know that he and Grannie had enjoyed their copy together.

"Let it be known," Billy started on the first chapter. "That this is the story of the Cross family, and it shall be known as "A Cross to Bear.""

Before You Go...

HELP AN AUTHOR

write a review

THANK YOU!

Share your voice and help guide other readers to these wonderful books. Even if it's only a line or two, your reviews help readers discover the author's books so they can continue creating stories that you'll love. Log in to your favorite retailer and leave a review. Thank you.

AWARD WINNING, BESTSELLING AUTHOR

Kathi Barton, a winner of the Pinnacle Book Achievement Award and a best-selling author on Amazon and All Romance books, lives in Nashport, Ohio, with her husband, Paul. When not creating new worlds and romance, Kathi and her husband enjoy camping and going to auctions. She can also be seen at county fairs with her husband, an artist and potter.

Her muse, a cross between Jimmy Stewart and Hugh Jackman, brings her stories to life for her readers in a way that has them coming back time and again for more. Her favorite genre is paranormal romance, with a great deal of spice. You can visit Kathi online and drop her an email if you'd like. She loves hearing from her fans. aaronskiss@gmail.com.

Follow Kathi on her blog: http://kathisbartonauthor.blogspot.com/